Cover Art by T.K. Chapin

This book is a work of fiction. Characters and events are the product of the author's imagination and used fictitiously. Any resemblance to persons living or dead, places, events or locales is purely coincidental.

Published by Sweet Dreams Publications
First Edition, 2018
Published in the United States of America

Contact information:
Mary Manners: sunriserun63@aol.com

~ Dedication ~

To Dave Manners…
You are a true champion of the Father.

The 21 books that form The Potter's House series are linked by the theme of Hope, Redemption, and Second Chances. They are all stand-alone books and can be read in any order. Books will become progressively available from February 27, 2018

Book 1: The Homecoming, by Juliette Duncan

Book 2: When it Rains, T.K. Chapin

Book 3: Heart Unbroken, by Alexa Verde

Book 4: Long Way Home, by Brenda S Anderson

Book 5: Promises Renewed, By Mary Manners

Book 6: A Vow Redeemed, by Kristen M. Fraser

Book 7: Restoring Faith, by Marion Ueckermann

Books 8 – 21 coming throughout 2019

"Above all, love each other deeply, because love covers over a multitude of sins."

~ 1 Peter 4:8 ~

1

JACKSON REED SLID THE DOUBLE TURKEY and cheddar sandwich onto his plate, added a fistful of rippled potato chips, and hobbled into the living room, leaving his crutches behind. The metal pair gaped at him through the doorway, hideous annoyances that had stolen his dignity and pride. He'd walk without them again for good, starting right now, if it killed him.

And it just might.

His knee screamed with each step. Doc said the pain would ease with time, but grueling therapy sessions left him exhausted. He recalled his dad's words from their phone conversation last night. "Buck up, Jack. Wrap your mind around the pain, work through it. You know the drill."

Yeah, he knew the drill, all right. Dad had ingrained the demanding work ethic into him from the age of six, when he'd suited up in pads and a helmet and stepped onto turf for the first time in West Knoxville's peewee league. No whining, no complaining. Just get in there and get the job done.

That mindset had taken him to the top—a full ride to the University of Tennessee followed by a lucrative NFL contract with the Jaguars. The money poured in and he rode a promising wave of fame.

Until he blew out his right knee taking a late hit during the fourth quarter of a playoff game three months ago. Surgery followed, and his prognosis and NFL future were still up in the air.

Jackson massaged the sore knee over a ridge of scar, willing it to heal faster. He should feel better by now.

He bit off a chunk of the sandwich and punched a button on the remote to turn up the TV's volume. Mid-day news blared from the flat screen in full surround sound. A familiar voice danced across the room. He glanced up and choked on a mouthful of sandwich.

Brianna gazed at him, her eyes rich chocolate almonds set in a face like smooth cream. Her hair was shorter than he remembered, kissing her shoulders in a sassy blonde blunt cut. Her lips, perfectly glossed with a hint of color, just the way he liked them, moved to answer the announcer's questions.

"We're raising money to fund programming at Thursday's Child." Her voice was a smooth melody. The slight southern cadence warmed him, and he imagined it worked magic on the viewing audience as well. "There are so many children who need a supervised, safe place to spend quality time. Our goal at Thursday's Child is to get kids off the streets and into supervised activities where they can acquire skills that will enhance their quality of life."

"And you're currently sponsoring an auction?" The announcer leaned closer. Jackson figured he was trying to cop a look at Brianna's perky cleavage. His face burned, but he didn't know why he found the idea so annoying, so...personally degrading.

"Yes. But it's not your typical auction. You see, we've elicited the help of a dozen eligible bachelors and bachelorettes in the Knoxville area who've each agreed to donate an evening's date to his or her highest bidder." A host of photos flashed across the screen. Jackson gasped. Brianna stared back at him from one of the featured snapshots, her dark eyes framed by naturally-lush lashes. She was even more beautiful than he remembered. "The auction opened just a few minutes ago, at noon. We encourage people to go online, to the Thursday's Child website, to place their bids. The auction will close this Thursday at midnight and we'll announce the lucky winners on Friday's evening edition of Channel Ten News."

Jackson sprang from the chair and hobbled over to the coffee table. He barely felt the pain that sliced through his knee as he bent over an open laptop and punched in the Internet address of Thursday's Child's website that scrolled across the bottom of the

TV screen. He kept his gaze glued to the TV as the website popped up. He couldn't take his eyes off Brianna.

"I'll have to check my savings account." The announcer grinned at Brianna and Jackson felt his gut twist. "A date with you is sure to be a real treat. Thank you for joining us." The leach turned from Brianna to face the camera full on. "That was Brianna Caufield with Thursday's Child. Back to you, Susan."

Jackson turned his attention to the webpage. He clicked on a link and quickly scanned the information posted. Brianna already had three bids, the highest a measly one-hundred dollars. He quickly jabbed a few buttons and sat back, satisfied.

****

Brianna pushed back from the interview desk. She couldn't get away from the announcer quick enough. What a creep. She prayed his piggy bank was on life support. She couldn't imagine spending an evening in his company, even to benefit Thursday's Child. She tugged the wireless microphone box Renee had tucked into the waistband of her linen pencil skirt and disentangled the clip from her blouse. "Did I do okay?"

"You were awesome." Renee took the microphone. "The pledges have already started pouring in. Take a look."

Brianna bent over the laptop Renee had propped open on the counter. The wireless connection streamed a live image of Thursday's Child's auction webpage. She gasped and tapped the screen.

"What's this?"

Renee grinned. "Secret admirer, maybe?"

"That's a lot of money." A five-thousand dollar bid topped the three that had already been placed in her name—by forty-nine hundred dollars. "What's the guy's name?"

"Now, Brianna, you know that's confidential until the announcement of the winners." Renee winked and tucked a stray wisp of fiery red hair behind her ear. "The marketing department for the news team is remaining steadfastly silent. They won't even give *me* a hint, so I guess you'll just have to wait to find out like everybody else."

"Well...as long as it's not the creepy announcer over there, I'm good with it." Concerned for the safety of the participants, she'd been hesitant to buy into the auction idea at first. But Renee had promised a stringent screening process and Brianna trusted her. After all, they'd been best friends since their first day of college, when they shared a cramped dorm room at the University of Tennessee. "Someone with so much money to burn and a heart for our kids can't be all that bad. Five thousand dollars will go a long way toward funding our summer programs, and that's just one bid. Let's keep an eye on things and see what happens." She grabbed her purse and headed toward the door. "I'm going to take a quick run before I head back to the office to finish up some paperwork. You want to come?"

"Not today. I've got to take care of a few errands. I'll meet you back at the office later."

"Okay, later."

Brianna was glad for the solitude. Bradford pear trees were just coming into peak bloom along Cherokee Boulevard, and a host of birds chattered beneath brilliant sunshine. The air was warm and dry, the humidity low and perfect for a quick, mind-numbing run. She laced up her tennis shoes and tucked the Kia's ignition key into the hidden pocket of her navy running shorts.

She slipped easily into a rhythm along the quiet street. Mild spring air coaxed flowering shrubs and colorful bulbs to life. She wondered what it must be like to live in one of the massive, upscale houses that were nestled into meticulously landscaped lots the length of the boulevard. How must it feel to wake to such opulence each day? She wouldn't know. Her job as co-director and senior counselor of the Thursday's Child program left much to be desired in the form of monetary compensation for the many hours of blood, sweat, and tears she poured into the program. But the emotional rewards far exceeded what she could have ever imagined. She wouldn't trade a moment of lost free time, not a drop of perspiration, for the smiles she saw on the kids' faces and their excitement at hearing about a new rec league or art class.

A vision of Jackson, tall and tan the way he'd looked when things were good between them...before the lure of money and fame changed him...popped into her mind, and she would have kicked herself if she hadn't found the perfect stride, eased into a perfect pace. Back then he would have loved helping her at Thursday's Child.

In contrast, now he knew all about what it was like to live in the lap of luxury. He owned a house in Jacksonville, on the bank of the Saint John's River. She knew, because he'd been featured on a segment of *Homes of the Rich and Famous* last year.

And he had a loft apartment overlooking the river in downtown Knoxville, too, for when he came home during the off season to visit his father. She imagined it was just as lavish, since his last NFL contract had brought in several million dollars plus endorsements for the past year alone. His contract negotiations were reported in the Knoxville papers and a highlight of local radio news.

She wouldn't know first-hand, though, since they hadn't spoken in years.

Six years, to be exact.

Her breath caught at the thought of those final days they'd spent together, and she had to fight to maintain an even pace. She willed her arms to pump in an easy rhythm and kept her head up, gaze focused straight ahead. She still remembered the clean, woodsy smell of him when he held her close, the scent of cherry-flavored gum he chewed, and she wondered if he ever thought of her, or if he'd even care that today was the anniversary of her miscarriage...the day she'd lost her baby—their baby—six years ago. How could he? He didn't know...she hadn't told him she was pregnant. Oh, she'd wanted to, had every intention to.

But for weeks he'd gushed with news of the draft, and the fact that he'd been picked up by the Jaguars, until finally he was set to leave in a only a few days to report to camp. She held her breath, hoping he'd ask her to go with him, though that wouldn't have been a viable option anyway. But it would have been nice...would have made things just a bit better...had he asked.

But he didn't. So she kept the news of the baby to herself. Telling him would hold him here for all the wrong reasons. If he didn't want her, how would he feel about being tied down by a baby, too?

So she'd let him walk away, told him to go on with his life.

And he had.

Five weeks later, in the middle of an unseasonably chilly spring night—a Thursday night—she lost the baby. She'd named him Luke, and when she prayed for him, she called him by name.

And she asked God to forgive her single lapse in judgment, the only time she'd given in to Jackson's sweet talk and promises. Because, just like she'd known somewhere in the dark recesses of her soul at the time, it had led to heartache and loss.

Tears clouded her eyes. The memory still hurt, and the loss still overwhelmed. Days like today, when the breeze whispered sweet and mild with the laughter of children playing in the park along the boulevard, were especially hard. But she doubted Jackson even gave it a second thought, just like he hadn't given her a second thought when he'd stormed out without so much as a backward glance on that late-April day.

She came to a crossroad, glanced both ways for oncoming traffic. Nothing coming, so she eased across the street and over to the next leg of the running trail. She quickly switched gears and decided to go the full distance today and work this odd sense of disappointment from her gut. A good, long run always raised her spirits, and she hoped today would be no different.

She had an hour before Andy's school bus dropped him at her office at the Thursday's Child building. She'd meet him there, ask about his day. Not that he ever had more than two words to say when it came to school. "Okay" and "Fine" seemed to be the favorites. Maybe he wouldn't bring home a discipline referral from one of his teachers today—

another crumpled paper slashed by red pen that outlined the many facets of his insolence. She'd need to sign it and schedule another follow-up conference with the principal. They were on a first name basis with the way things were going.

"Avoid these referrals and save a tree," she'd told Andy when he brought one home just last week. A disagreement with his math teacher over a missing assignment was worth an hour-long detention. "Just do what your teachers ask. It's not that hard."

"Easy for you to say." He handed over the wadded paper he'd carelessly stuffed into the front pocket of his faded jeans and flipped coffee-with-heavy-cream hair from charcoal eyes to glance at her. The gesture reminded her of Terri, and she wondered how things were going in New York. She wouldn't know, since neither she nor Andy had heard from his mother—her older sister—in over two weeks. Anyway, Andy's hair was too long. It needed a cut—badly. Brianna frowned. Given the circumstances, that was a battle best saved for another day. "No one bosses you around all day long."

She rolled her eyes and smirked. "Just wait. You'll be an adult one day, too. Then you'll see it's not all it's cracked up to be."

"No way." His eyes widened in mortification. "I don't want to grow up. Grownups are crazy."

She couldn't blame him for feeling that way. Her sister had seemed to go off the deep end, leaving her only child to fend for himself while she chased her latest dream of becoming the next top New York fashion designer, since her last dream of movie stardom hadn't panned out. If Brianna hadn't intervened and brought Andy to live with her, he'd probably be another casualty of the streets. He was only twelve, after all, and he still needed a mother's touch.

Needless to say, he wasn't happy about having to leave his friends and everything else that was familiar back in California. And the fact that he'd been with Brianna for nearly two months now hadn't changed a thing. The boy was mad at the world, and she was at a loss as to how to soften his tough veneer. She prayed for a breakthrough soon.

Her mind wandered to Thursday's Child. Kids like Andy were the driving force behind the program—kids who were lost in the shuffle of adult irresponsibility, who needed a safe haven, a place to belong. But, not immune to the economy's current struggles, the program was in serious crisis. Even with a good turnout for the online auction, they'd fall short of paying next quarter's bills. The building's lease was up in August, and they'd either have to renegotiate the contract at a higher rate or buy the building and the grounds surrounding it outright. Neither was a viable option, given the current situation. What Thursday's Child needed was a benefactor with generous pockets, someone with the capital to set the program firmly on its feet. And it needed to happen soon. She couldn't bear to see the kids she'd grown to love tossed back out on the street.

Her thoughts turned to the high bid she'd drawn. She'd balked at the idea of putting herself up for auction. She had no desire to date, even if the date was merely in the name of raising money. But Renee had talked her into it. How would it look, after all, for her to recruit other eligible adults if she wasn't willing to put herself out there, as well? She grimaced. Renee could talk the paint off a wall if she set her mind to it.

But maybe Renee was right after all. Perhaps her anonymous bidder would turn out to be a prince charming with a million dollars to burn, and a real heart for her kids.

Yeah, and maybe the moon really *was* made of cheese.

2

AN ARMY OF ANGRY WASPS dive-bombed inside Brianna's belly. She sat dead-last in the row of bachelorettes, and the same creepy news anchor she'd had the pleasure of dealing with a few days ago made his way toward her, announcing the auction winners as he went. The half-dozen eligible bachelors had already been paired with their female bidders and all seemed reasonably pleased as they exited the studio to give the bachelorettes their turn to meet anxious mystery men. Now, each time a name was revealed, the high-bidding man came out to greet the bachelorette he'd 'won' for an evening on the town.

Oh, she hoped the anchor wouldn't reveal himself as the highest bidder for a date with *her*. The idea mortified her, and the mischievous gleam in his muddy-brown eyes was disturbing. She cringed at the thought and sent up a quick prayer for a more positive outcome. A date with anyone but him—anyone at all—and she'd be good with it.

Brianna wiggled freshly-painted toes in the strappy sandals that hugged her feet. The shoes were new, and a bit too tight, and she wished now she'd worn her older, comfortable pair with the little black knee-length sheath she'd found on sale at the mall. But she wanted to look her best, and if it meant nursing sore feet she'd just have to bite the bullet. If this auction went well, perhaps they'd make it an annual event. The total bids had climbed to a healthy five-figure amount, enough to get spring programs for the kids off to a promising start.

Now it was time to pay up, and she was determined to do her part. Visions of Lynette and Lucy, rambunctious eleven-year-old twin sisters with wheat-blonde hair and a spattering of freckles across their button noses, sprang into her head. They'd begun coming to the center a few weeks ago when their mom's nursing shift changed to evenings and their dad picked up extra overtime as a UPS delivery driver. Now, instead of riding the bus to an empty house each afternoon, they got dropped off at the center, where they found help with their homework and enjoyed supervised gym time with new friends.

The anchor stood two women away, and the rank odor of sweat laced the air. Brianna fought the urge to pinch her nose as he drew closer. She felt a little light-headed beneath the bright studio lights. They were *hot*, and annoying beads of moisture pooled at the nape of her neck as her heart galloped.

Oh, why had she ever let Renee talk her into this crazy scheme?

Because of the kids. She glanced at Andy, waiting in the wings to her left. He flashed a rare grin, thrilled as he shadowed the evening edition sportscaster through a private tour of the studio. Soon, he'd perform a mock-up newscast in front of the green screen while she sequestered with the sweaty anchor and his female co-anchor, like a prisoner on death-row awaiting her fate.

For kids like Andy. Yeah, she could do this. This was a walk in the park, compared to the challenges they faced on a daily basis. She drew a deep breath and willed her heart to stop racing. *Get a grip. Don't be a wimp.*

****

Jackson leaned against the studio wall to ease the weight off his aching knee. The painkillers he'd downed before leaving the apartment had kicked the pain back to a dull roar, but they made him feel a bit lightheaded.

Or maybe his head swam from the sight of Brianna on the monitor. She was a vision in a sassy little black sleeveless dress that offset sleek blonde hair and long, sculpted legs. She must still be an avid runner. No woman sported legs like that unless she worked for them.

He waited while the slim, dark-haired woman seated to the right of Brianna was introduced to her mystery date. Awkward smiles all around, a few murmured greetings, and they exited the stage together.

He was up next. It was a good thing he'd checked the auction site at the last minute. Some guy had outbid him by five hundred bucks. Imagine that! He made a statement by upping his bid to fifteen thousand, which ought to impress Brianna. It was an iron-clad number. He didn't know much—anything, really—about the organization she'd founded with her friend, Renee, called Thursday's Child, but he knew fifteen-K was a lot more than most people could afford to part with. No way would he get outbid tossing that kind of money around.

He watched the anchor lean into Brianna a little too closely. The guy had a smug look on his face and belly rolls like a Shar-Pei puppy. Something in his watery eyes told Jackson he thought *he* had won the bid. Well, wouldn't he be shocked?

Brianna would be shocked, too. Jackson's gut suddenly clenched and his knee throbbed. Maybe this was a mistake. After all, they hadn't seen each other in more than six years, hadn't so much as spoken a handful of words since that awful night.

He'd been such a jerk to her. Even now, beads of sweat broke out along his forehead as words echoed through his mind.

"Talk to me, Jackson." Brianna's chocolate-kiss eyes melted into a pool of tears. "I thought you had another week before you had to leave."

"I do…but I should go now. I need to get settled in, clear my head." He'd turned away from her and set his gaze to the mountains in the distance, turning smoky-pink beneath a dusky sky. "Besides, I'm suffocating here, Bri."

"Suffocating?" She choked on the word. "What's that supposed to mean?"

"You're putting too much pressure on me, Brianna. I can't love you the way you want me to—need me to. I've just got too much on my plate right now."

He watched her flinch as if he'd struck her, heard the sharp intake of breath.

"So that's how it is, Jackson? After everything we've shared I'm nothing more than another item on your overflowing plate?" She strode around to plant herself in front of him.

One glance at the tears cascading down her cheeks had him wishing he could take back the words. "I just mean—"

"Forget it, Jackson. You've made it perfectly clear how you feel." She turned her back to him and crossed her arms over her belly. The tremble in her shoulders matched her voice. "Just go, then. Your plate is clean, at least as far as I'm concerned. I don't want to be a burden to you."

The riffling of papers drew him back to the present, and realization smacked him like a sucker-punch. This wasn't the football field he was playing on, and the studio crowd hadn't come to watch him run his famous million dollar plays. This was a benefit for underprivileged kids, something obviously close to Brianna's heart. What was he thinking, coming here trying to buy his way into a date with her?

He forced back the bile that rose in his throat. *Good grief, what have I done?*

****

Brianna wished the anchor would stop panting. His breath smelled like boiled eggs beneath the bright, hot studio lights. It was amazing just how much the TV could hide.

She drew a deep breath and held it when he stepped in front of her. He shuffled a handful of crisp index-sized cue cards scribbled with notes as his leering gaze met hers. His voice dripped with suspense. "Brianna Caufield, co-founder of Thursday's Child, are you ready to meet your date?"

"I...um..." *About as ready as I am to have a root canal without anesthesia. Note to self: Have it out with Renee at the first opportunity.*

He glanced at the cue-cards, and his smile suddenly turned under, like a sail deflating. His eyes narrowed and his nose did a rabbit scrunch as he muttered, "This can't be right."

The female co-anchor gave him a not-so-gentle nudge and leaned over to glance at the card, which he promptly removed from her view. She urged, "Hey, the suspense is killing us, Art. Who's the lucky guy?"

He drew a ragged breath as he plastered on a billboard smile and stared directly into the camera. His voice held steady, unlike the trembling hand that clenched into a fist at his side, out of the camera's view. "Why, he's none other than Knoxville's very own hometown hero, the all-star quarterback who once led the University of Tennessee to an SEC championship and a Sugar Bowl win." He gestured dramatically toward the wings and threw his arms wide. "Jackson Reed, come on out. Your generous fifteen-thousand dollar bid has won you a date with the beautiful Brianna Caufield."

Brianna lurched in her seat. *Jackson Reed...no, it can't be. Wake up, wake up!*

The room began to whirl and harsh lights danced before Brianna's eyes. She blinked hard once, twice, and heard a flurry of movement to her left. Then *he* strode out. He had to duck to clear a microphone suspended from the ceiling, and his height shaded the lights, easing the glare that burned her eyes. His dark hair was a bit shorter than she remembered, but it still fell in tousled waves across intense, smoky-gray eyes.

The years had added muscle—lots of it. And he flashed the same 'I can get out of anything' grin that had melted her the first time they'd met, back in the school lunchroom in sixth grade, when he'd tried to swap his warm, stinky tuna fish on squashed white bread for the turkey and cheddar on wholegrain her mom had packed along with juicy red seedless grapes and a homemade frosted fudge brownie. Well, that grin wouldn't work its magic on her anymore. No way in...

"Hello, Brianna."

Her insides turned to ice. His voice was deep, coaxing, just as she remembered. She sat paralyzed, speechless. Every thought flew from her mind. She gripped the armrests of the chair like life preservers on a sinking Titanic.

"What's wrong with her?" Andy's sneakers thumped the studio floor and the room rocked wildly as she tried to stand.

"Somebody catch her." The co-anchor rushed over to fan her face with a cue card. "Bring some water, Art. Hurry, let's go to commercial break."

****

"You're Jackson Reed." Andy's eyes grew round with amazement as he followed Jackson down the hall.

"Yeah, that's right."

They made their way to the lobby of the news studio, on the parking level. Outside, rush-hour traffic raced up and down Kingston Pike as people scurried home from work.

"For real." Andy's voice grated on Brianna's nerves like rough-grade sandpaper. She wished he'd just be quiet and keep walking. "You're really him. Wow, can I have your autograph?"

"Sure." Jackson had the audacity to grin. "How about a picture, too?"

Andy paused to rock back on his heels. "You have a camera?"

"On my cell phone." He pulled out the latest hi-tech model, one that would have set Brianna back two week's salary.

"Cool." Andy turned to her. "Aunt Brianna, toss me a pen and some paper from your purse."

"No." She shook her head, clutching the handbag to her chest. She still felt warm and a bit nauseated, as if her insides were filled with chili peppers. "Not now, Andy. Go wait in the car."

His eyes clouded with confusion. "But—"

"I said, not now." She fumbled through the purse and tossed him the car keys. "You remember where we parked?"

"Of course. Right beside that sweet red Mustang." He turned to Jackson. "Hey, is that your Mustang?"

"Maybe...yes."

"Wow. Can I sit in it? I'll bet you've got an awesome stereo. I'll bet—"

Brianna stomped one spike-heeled foot and pointed toward the door. "Andy—the car—now. And don't get any ideas. Just unlock it and get in. I'll be out in a minute."

He sighed. "Radio?"

"Yes, turn it on. But nothing else."

"Whatever." He tossed the keys into the air, caught them with a jangle before heading through automatic double doors into the parking lot. He turned back to Jackson before the doors slipped closed. "Can I get an autograph later?"

"Sure, and we'll play some ball, too, okay?"

"Promise?"

"You bet."

"Cool." There was a bounce in Andy's step as he loped toward the Kia.

"You shouldn't have told him that." Brianna's cheeks burned as she watched him unlock the passenger door and slide in. "You shouldn't make promises you don't plan to keep."

"Who said I don't plan to keep my promise?"

"Prior history, Jackson." She strode across the room, arms crossed in a death grip. "A less-than-pristine track record."

"Brianna, please." He limped after her. She took pity, slowed a step or two. And it irked her that she should feel any sympathy for him whatsoever. He'd certainly shown her none when she'd needed it the most. "I shouldn't have blindsided you. I—"

"Save the football terminology. You had no right to do this, Jackson." Her chin came up, and she was mortified when her bottom lip began to tremble. She bit down hard, drew a breath. "Thousands of men live in this town. Thousands of men have the Internet and money—okay, maybe not *that* kind of money. Anyway, why did it have to be *you*?"

"It was an honest bid. I'm just trying to help you out."

She crossed her arms again, glared at him.

"Okay, okay. I saw you on TV and I just...well, I thought..."

Irritation danced up Brianna's spine. It made her uncomfortable to see him squirm. On TV, when he was interviewed after games, he always sounded so sure, so in control. Jackson Reed was *the* man every woman in America wanted...everyone but her. "I'll take the money, Jackson. It will go a long way towards funding our upcoming programs for the Thursday's Child kids. But the date with you—well—no. It's just not going to happen."

"So you're reneging on a deal?" He shook his head and his eyes narrowed with disappointment.

Brianna bowed up. "Call it what you want. I'm not going on a date with you, Jackson. No way." His guilt trip certainly wouldn't work on her. Maybe six years ago...but not now.

"I never knew you to be a quitter, Bri."

That fueled the fire. "You want to talk about quitting? Take a look in the mirror, Jackson."

A hand flew to cover his chest. "Ouch, you wound me."

"Save the theatrics for your post-game interviews."

"Wow." He removed his suit jacket and tugged loose the tie that appeared to strangle him. Muscles tensed beneath a navy form-fitting button-down dress shirt that deepened the gray of his eyes. He'd lost that little-boy look, the lankiness that had followed him through high school and most of college, but his eyes still radiated familiar mischief beneath tufts of dark hair she used to love running her fingers through. She forced her gaze away, swallowed hard and lowered her eyes to the strappy sandals that had her feet screaming with a full-blown ache. "No comment."

"Suits me just fine." She spun on one heel and turned her back to him. "Andy's waiting for me. I have to go."

"But we're not finished here."

She halted mid-stride, swung back to glare at him. “Oh, we’re finished, Jackson. We were finished that night you walked out on me. You remember that, don’t you?”

His gaze flickered, and his eyes darkened from smoky gray to coal-black in an instant. “How could I forget?” He reached into the back pocket of his neatly-pressed khakis and pulled out a piece of paper. With a flourish, he unfolded it and muttered under his breath as he scanned the small print. “Here it is, in plain black and white.” His gaze rose to challenge hers. “Read it for yourself, if you don’t believe me.”

“What?”

He jabbed the paper with an index finger. “Says right here in the fine print—no date, no payment.” He turned the paper to show her, and a smug grin accompanied the tapping. “So, what’s it gonna be, Bri?”

“You mean...?” She gaped at him in disbelief. Surely, he couldn’t be serious. She felt like ripping the paper from his hand and shredding it, but stifled the urge by drawing a deep breath and counting to five very slowly. When she spoke, the calm tone of her voice masked the rage building like a tidal wave about to unleash its fury. “You’d do that, wouldn’t you? Take back what you’ve already given?”

Just like he’d done before—when he left her twisting in the wind, her heart shattered on the ground in a million aching pieces. It seemed to be the Jackson Reed trademark move.

"Just one date, Bri." His eyes were pleading, and he jammed one hand into the pocket of his khakis. "What we have...isn't finished."

"What we *had*—" She enunciated the word, "—*is* finished." She bit her bottom lip, felt her eyes burn with tears that were fighting to punch their way out. "But I can't let you take all that money back. Thursday's Child needs it. The *kids* need it." She turned away for a moment, drew another deep, cleansing breath and closed her eyes, prayed for strength and the patience to refrain from ripping his head off right there in the lobby.

I can do all things through Christ who strengthens me. The words washed over her, calmed her, gently reminded her who she was...who she'd become during the six years he'd been gone.

"Okay, Jackson. Have it your way. But not tonight—no date tonight." She eyed the parking lot, where Andy sang along with the radio blasting at full volume. If she didn't get out of there quick, the police were libel to respond to a disturbing the peace complaint. "Call the Thursday's Child office tomorrow. The number's in the phone book. A bright guy like you should have no problem finding it. Ask for Renee. She'll set things up. Now, I really have to go."

She didn't wait for a reply. The spiky heels on her sandals spat like gunfire across polished tile as she strode through double-glass doors without so much as a glance back.

Safe in the car with the radio lowered to a reasonable volume, her breath escaped in a loud gush. She'd call Renee as soon as she got home, lay down stringent guidelines. If Jackson wanted to hold his donation ransom in exchange for a date, he'd get his date. One date...something during daylight hours...in a heavily populated area...safe.

One date...and nothing more.

3

WELL, HE'D CERTAINLY MADE A mess of things.

Jackson sighed as he watched Brianna drive from the parking lot. She gunned the Kia's engine a little too hard, pulled into traffic a little too fast—certainly not setting a great example for the towheaded kid riding shotgun. And it was his fault.

He'd managed to hurt her—again.

He rubbed his chin, felt the five-o'clock shadow that had sprung to life along his jaw. Maybe he'd just mail his check into the Thursday's Child office and forget the whole date thing. After all, he didn't need to pay for a date, or force a female into one. He had a mile-long line waiting at the Jaguar's locker room, women throwing themselves at him every time he left the field after practice or a game. It was almost comical.

But Brianna was different...always had been. Their friendship went way back. She was the first kid he talked to when he transferred schools in the sixth grade. And over the years, what began as an awkward friendship became more...so much more. What had he been thinking to act like such an idiot the night he'd walked out on her? Sure, back then he had nothing to offer her but hopes and a farfetched dream. She'd needed more, wanted more—she'd certainly made that clear—and he didn't have it to give. There was nothing secure in his pursuit of an NFL career, no guarantees of what tomorrow might bring. And she'd longed for security. So he'd left—just like that.

The years of rough games and two-a-day workouts—and now this irritating knee injury—had proven just how unstable his career choice could be. Maybe he'd never play again. The doc just couldn't say for sure either way. Being sidelined had given him plenty of time to think. He was home now, and things were different.

He cranked up the stereo, slipped in his favorite CD to drown out memories of the way Brianna had looked that last day, when they'd argued in the common area of the dorm as thunder rumbled in the distance and heat lightning flashed the warning of an impending storm. Tears had muddied her pretty chocolate-almond eyes and streamed down cheeks that caught fire with the hurt.

His knee throbbed in time to the music from the stereo, but he ignored the pain. He needed a muscle-burning workout, something to take his mind off the mess he'd made. Just because his knee refused to cooperate was no reason to neglect his upper body, his throwing arm. He pulled into traffic along Kingston Pike and headed toward the gym.

Nothing like a pump-till-you-drop workout to make the mind go blank, clear the head and chase away bad memories.

****

"What was that all about?" Andy's eyes narrowed as he studied Brianna's white knuckles on the steering wheel. "You want me to drive? You're really stressed out."

"You can't drive. You're only twelve."

He bowed up. "I'm *almost* thirteen. Besides, Mom lets me drive all the time."

Her gaze left the road long enough to throw him a disbelieving look. "She *does not*."

"Wanna bet?" His smug expression told her otherwise. "Call her."

She would if it might do any good. But all she'd get is voicemail, and Terri hadn't responded to any of her messages for nearly two weeks. It was as if she'd fallen off the face of the earth. Brianna wasn't worried. The behavior was typical Terri. She'd call when she was ready, show up again when she felt the urge. "Well, you're here now, and you're not driving until you're legal. That's—"

"Seven-hundred and ninety-two more days." He flipped shaggy hair over his forehead to hide his eyes. "Make that, seven-hundred and ninety-two more *unbearably long* days."

"You've got that figured out? What's up with the D in math, then?"

He shrugged and punched a button on the stereo. A heavy rap beat rocked the car. "I dunno. Mr. Grinstead doesn't like me. Nobody here likes me."

"I like you." Brianna lowered the volume to a respectable level and jabbed the station pre-sets until a smooth melody soothed the growing ache in her head.

"That doesn't count. You *have* to like me. You're my aunt, remember?"

"How could I forget?" She flashed him a strained smile and shook her head ever-so-slightly as he reached to change the station again.

"I am not up for a station war today. Leave the music alone, please."

He grimaced but backed off. "You call that music? It's like vomit in my ears." He slumped resignedly in the seat.

"Sorry. It'll grow on you."

"Like poison ivy."

She sighed and eased her grip on the wheel.

Her fingers were beginning to tingle from a lack of circulation. "I'll bet your grades would improve if you did your homework more and talked in class less. I had Mr. Grinstead for math when I was in seventh grade. He's not so bad."

"You had him? Wow, he must be really old."

"Thanks, buddy. I feel a whole lot better now."

"Sorry. But he must be at least eighty. And he smells like moth balls and tells bad jokes that only he laughs at."

"He's not eighty. Maybe fifty-five or so, but certainly not eighty. And, yes, I guess he did tell some pretty awful jokes." She merged into traffic along I-40. "But you'll survive the class—I promise. I did, and Jackson had him, too."

"Jackson Reed?" His eyes grew wide with disbelief. "*You* went to school with Jackson Reed—*the* Jackson Reed?"

Oh, why had she opened that can of worms? Brianna hid a grimace.

"I sure did. We were in the same classes from sixth grade on." She'd give him that much, if it would motivate him—anything to keep his focus on schoolwork and off trouble. She kept the part about how she and Jackson had passed notes to each other during lectures, and how he'd asked her out for the first time by tossing her a note while Mr. Grinstead worked out scale-factor problems on the overhead. There was no need to tell him they'd skipped rocks at a hidden pond they'd found while taking a shortcut home from school one afternoon, and that Jackson could make his rock skim the surface of the water, skipping a dozen times, before it finally sank to the muddy bottom.

"Cool. Really, *really* cool. I'll bet he hated math, too."

"No, he was actually very good at math." He'd helped her survive calculus, and she'd guided him through his senior research paper for honors English. "Andy, you know if you don't get your grades up, you can't go out for spring practice with the football team."

"You mean you'll let me go?" He brushed waves of hair from his eyes and she saw them brighten with excitement. "You'll drive me to the field every day and pick me up when practice is finished?"

"Of course I will. Why wouldn't I?"

He shrugged. "I dunno. Mom never did. She was always too busy going to auditions and hanging out with that weird wannabe director dude. That's why I got kicked off the team—I couldn't make all the practices."

"Well, this is different." She pulled into their neighborhood and wound around to the driveway of their small frame house. The wrap-around porch could use a fresh coat of paint. Maybe she'd keep Andy busy with the project now that the weather was warming into full-blown spring. She groaned at the flower beds along the porch. Weeds had taken up residence and owned the whole zip code. Brianna sighed and shook her head as she drove into the garage and cut the engine. Weeds were the least of her problems; she had more pressing worries at the moment. "You get your grades up and I'll take you to every practice. That's a promise, Andy. Deal?"

He flipped the hair back again, studied her with cautious charcoal eyes beneath the warm glow of the garage door light. "You mean it?"

She gave him a reassuring smile. "Yes, I mean it. A promise is a promise. No take-backs."

"Even so..." He reached for her hand. "Can we shake on it?"

"Of course, if it makes you feel better." She grasped his hand, gave it a shake that would make any ironman proud. "Just one more thing."

He groaned and flopped back against the seat. "I knew this was coming. What?"

"You can keep the rock star hair until practice starts. Then it gets cut."

"But—"

She shook her head. "No buts about it, buddy. The hair goes. You can grow it back when the season is over, if you still want to."

He grimaced and ran a hand from brow to nape like she planned on scalping him instead of just trimming the hair. "Okay. I can deal. I don't like it, but I can deal."

"Good. Now go on in and feed Max, then start on that pile of schoolwork you carted home this afternoon. I'll be there in a few minutes to help you, if you need it. I have to make a call."

"Is it about Jackson Reed? Sweet! He said he'd toss a football with me. Maybe he'll help me with my game, too. When do you think we can see him again? Tomorrow?"

Brianna's belly soured. If she had her way, she'd never see him again. But she had the kids at Thursday's child to consider, and now Andy was swept up, as well. She sighed.

"Go inside, Andy. Fill Max's food dish and make sure he has plenty of fresh water. Then it's straight to the table with all your books. No detours to the fridge—or the computer. Do your homework, pronto."

"Yes, Ma'am." He saluted her smartly and slid from the car. "But Jackson Reed...wow!"

He clomped up the stairs and through the back door, slamming it in the way she'd become familiar with. Brianna groaned and settled back in the seat. She pinched the bridge of her nose to stave off the migraine that threatened to crack her skull wide open, and slipped off the sandals that gnawed tender flesh at her ankles.

Ah...peace and quiet—finally. She closed her eyes and leaned her head against the seat. Oh, how she longed for a power nap. It wouldn't hurt to indulge for a few blissful moments. Then she'd get back to the business at hand.

Ugh...homework. And dinner. She couldn't forget about dinner. Andy wouldn't dream of missing a meal. The kid plowed through food like a freight train. She'd have to throw something together, and quick. She glanced at her watch—nearly seven o'clock already. Maybe Andy wouldn't mind macaroni and cheese...again. She could steam some broccoli for a side. Yeah, that would go over well. He'd gobble it right up and beg for seconds.

Her purse began to vibrate on the console beside her. She groaned and delved through the mess inside for her cell phone. A quick check of the caller ID told her Renee was on the other end. She flipped open the phone.

"Oh, Brianna. I'm so sorry." Renee's voice rushed through the line. "I had no idea your date was...*him*. Where are you? Are you okay? You bolted from the studio like the place was on fire."

"Slow down." Her head throbbed and she pressed two fingers to her left temple to massage in slow, tight circles. "One question at a time, please."

"We can fix this...somehow. I'll get right on it. I feel like it's all my fault."

"It's not your fault, Renee. Who would have ever imagined Jackson would pull a stunt like this...after all this time."

"Oh, Bri. Maybe there's a loophole. You might not have to actually go on a *date* with him in order for Thursday's Child to keep the money."

"I've already checked the fine print...and the date is a requirement. There's no way around it. The legal team wrote some iron-clad rules."

"Then maybe we can make ends meet without Jackson's bid. I'll stay up late and crunch some numbers."

"You know that's impossible. Even with his money, we'll be cutting it too close for comfort." Brianna bit back an onslaught of accusing words. If Renee hadn't come up with this hair-brained idea...

But she couldn't blame her friend. After all, she'd agreed to the auction, too. Besides, Renee had been there for her through the darkest times...when Jackson left and then, later, when she lost Luke. She'd nursed Brianna back to health, both physically and emotionally. And she'd been an angel last year, too, when Brianna's dad suffered a massive stroke and died a few days later.

Brianna backpedaled. "I mean, I know we need the money. We can't keep Thursday's Child running without it. And we've worked too hard to quit now. Think of the kids, Renee."

She sighed. "I *am* thinking of them. But I'm thinking of you, too, Bri."

"I'll be okay. Just don't say a word to anyone about...well, you know, Renee. Just don't, okay?" She'd told no one at Thursday's Child about what had happened between her and Jackson. Renee was the only one in the world who knew her secret, and

Brianna planned to keep things that way. It was nobody's business but hers...and God's. And she'd made peace with the mistakes she'd made so long ago, when she was in that in-between place...no longer child, but not yet adult, either.

"We need to talk." Renee's voice rushed over the phone. "If you're determined to go through with this, we need to come up with a plan. I don't want to see you get hurt again. I can't bear it."

"Not tonight." Brianna was tired to the bone. The last thing she wanted was to revive the heartache of the past. "Not now. I have to help Andy with his math homework. And I haven't even started dinner."

"You can't put this off, Brianna. I'll run by that little Italian restaurant by the river and pick up one of their pasta specials. You know how much you love their baked spaghetti. And I can give Andy a hand with his math, too. Word problems are my specialty, after all. I'll be there in twenty minutes. Put on a pot of coffee."

"Renee, wait—" The line went dead.

****

Later that night Brianna sighed and rolled over to stare at the ceiling, pulling the covers up over her chin. Sleep refused to come, though she was flat-out bone-tired. Her mind raced and wandered through memories and places best forgotten.

She massaged her left ring finger where a pale band of flesh once stood out bright as the summer sun against tanned skin when she removed the promise ring Jackson gave her their sophomore year in college. He was going to marry her one day, he'd said, and he wanted her to have the token until he could save enough for a decent engagement ring—something glittery and substantial and fit for a woman with her beauty. And oh, she'd believed him.

Now the promise ring was tucked in her bottom dresser drawer, among stacks of running shorts and T-shirts from the slew benefit road races she'd participated in over the years. She'd wrapped the delicate silver that held her birthstone in tissue paper and slid it into a zippered baggie, and she rarely thought about it.

Except for now, when she knew Jackson was just across town, most likely swapping stories with some of his football buddies while they caught whatever sport played on the big-screen TV down at Bailey's. He always did like hanging out at Bailey's.

She had, too, in more carefree and reckless days. But times had changed her...grief and loss had changed her. Now she spent her Friday nights planning events for the center with Renee, or counseling troubled teens who simply needed someone to listen, to care.

Max sighed and stretched his massive black-lab legs from where he lay on the floor beside her bed. His head came up and dark, soulful eyes studied her. She'd rescued him from the local shelter nearly five years ago, nursed him back from a pitiful case of mange and heartworms, and now they seemed to understand each other more than most married couples.

"Having trouble sleeping, too?" She asked as she leaned over the side of the bed to scratch behind his ears. "How about we read a little? I can go over the schedule for this summer's rec leagues. That ought to do the trick."

Max grumbled and tucked his front paws beneath his chin as if to say, "If you really have to, I guess it's okay."

Brianna switched on the bedside lamp. Pale light washed over the room as she reached for the notebook she'd set on the night table. A bit of work-related reading would force all thoughts of Jackson from her mind—she hoped.

4

"A LITTLE FARTHER. COME ON, give it some gas." Jackson glanced into the pickup's rearview mirror to see Brianna wave him back. "A little to the left. That's good. Stop." She held out her hand like a very serious but cute traffic cop.

He tapped the brake, shut off the truck's engine, and leaned out the driver's window. "You want us to dump it all here?"

"Well, not just *dump* it." Her eyes widened with mortification. "You'll crush the seedlings the kids worked so hard to transplant."

"I get the picture." He motioned to the truck bed, filled with bags of mulch that had been donated by a local home improvement store. "You know, it would have been a lot easier to have dumped the mulch first and then planted the seedlings."

"Yes, I know." Defensive, one hand went to her hip and her lips pursed into a tight frown. "But we didn't have mulch donated at the time, and we needed to get the plants in before spring turned into summer."

"Don't worry." It was hard to keep a straight face when she looked so ticked off. "We'll get the job done right."

"Good." She was already retreating, her feet like pedals pumping backwards, away from him. "I'm going around back to help the kids with the flower beds that flank the parking lot."

Of course she was. She'd go to Siberia to get away from him, no doubt. She'd made that much clear when they'd negotiated this 'date'.

Some date...he was sweating his hind end off hauling what felt like tons of mulch while the towheaded kid who'd mauled him the other night for an autograph rode shotgun and talked nonstop. *And* he'd brought a digital camera, to boot. He'd snapped so many shots Jackson was beginning to feel like a contestant on *America's Next Top Model.*

He sighed and raised his voice a decibel or two so Brianna could hear him as she rounded the corner of the building and disappeared from his sight. "I'll go back to the home improvement store for the next load as soon as we've laid these."

"Great," she shouted back. "They've donated a hundred bags. I hope that'll be enough to cover every bed."

A hundred bags...good grief!

He took mental inventory. At twenty-five bags per load, it would take him four trips to transport the entire donation here. Good thing the home improvement center was just a few miles down the road. Jackson shook his head. How had he gotten roped into this?

Oh, yeah. The auction. This was some date he'd negotiated. And why?

Hmmm...Brianna's chocolate eyes, her sweet pucker of a mouth. And those long, toned legs. Yeah, that had something to do with it.

A *lot* to do with it. She could coax wax to melt.

"I'll help." The kid—Andy was his name—scrambled from the passenger seat and ran around to the back of the truck. The tailgate clattered as he tugged and lifted. "You should rest your knee, Mr. Reed."

"Jackson." The *mister* stuff made him feel ancient. He slipped from the driver's seat and tested his knee, bit back an oath and struggled to ignore the shooting pain. No way would he let this scrawny kid outwork him when it came to hauling mulch—or anything else, for that matter. "Hey, those bags are awfully heavy. Don't hurt yourself."

"Who, me?" The kid's eyebrows knit together in a scowl. "I'm stronger than I look."

"Sure, you are."

Bent on proving it, Andy reached into the truck bed, grabbed a forty pound bag, and hauled it out. He tossed it on the ground at Jackson's feet. "I beat up a kid twice my size last month."

"Oh, yeah?" Jackson watched him scramble into the truck bed for another bag. "What for?"

"He was mad at Aunt Brianna because she caught him sneaking a smoke behind the center and took his cigarettes away. We got into it the next day at school when he called her a—"

"Whoa." Jackson held up a hand. "You don't have to repeat it. I get the picture."

"Anyway, I got in-school suspension for three days, but he did, too. *And* I gave him a sweet-looking shiner. So it was worth it."

"What did Brianna have to say about that?"

"Oh…" A frown covered his face. "She told me to keep my eyes in my textbooks and my mouth closed and to let her fight her own battles. She gave me a big lecture about staying out of trouble—for the millionth time. She's really good at that kind of thing. My ears rang by the time she finished, and I wished the ground would swallow me up."

"She's pretty tough, huh?"

"I'll say. I got grounded, like, forever. I couldn't play basketball here at the center for a whole week and I had to clean the bathrooms instead. Have you ever had to clean a public bathroom?"

"Can't say I have."

"It was beyond disgusting."

"I'll bet." He hauled out a bag of mulch, tossed it toward the flower bed, and reached for another. "Where are your parents?"

Andy paused, shrugged. His eyes narrowed and darkened. "I dunno where my dad is. He and my mom never got married, and he took off when I was three. I barely remember him, but I don't care."

Oh, man. Tender subject.

"My mom's gone kind of...I don't know." He raised an index finger to make a circular motion beside his ear as he gnawed his lower lip. "She's in New York designing weird-looking clothes for anorexic runway models."

"Sounds...interesting."

He shrugged again, then took his frustration out on a bag of mulch. "I guess...if you like that kind of stuff. Me—I like football."

"I'm with you there."

"How old were you when you started playing?"

"Six. My dad took me out to the peewee league in West Knoxville."

"Oh." He ran a hand through sweaty caramel hair, left a streak of dirt across his forehead. "I'm almost thirteen and I haven't gotten to play much. My mom...uh..." He lifted another bag, tossed it as if it didn't weigh nearly half of what he did. "Aunt Brianna said she'd get me to all the practices and the coach wants me, so..."

"Don't sweat it...Andy, right?"

He beamed. "Yeah."

"You look like you're a quick learner. Let's get this job done, and we'll toss the ball around, see what you've got."

"Cool."

Jackson dangled the truck keys. "I think we've dumped enough mulch at this bed. How about you drive what's left of the load to that one over there?" He motioned a hundred yards away, across the grass to the far side of the building.

The kid's eyes lit up. "You mean it?"

"Sure. It's a straight shot, and this isn't exactly I-40 at rush hour." In fact, his was the only truck in sight and the rest of the kids were busy working around the back of the building with Brianna.

"Aunt Brianna will pitch a fit. She thinks I'm too young to drive."

"I'd agree, if we were on the street. But we're not, and I'll ride shotgun just in case a semi happens to ride up on the lawn and try to take us out."

"If you say so." He grabbed the keys and jumped into the driver's seat before Jackson had a chance to change his mind. "But you don't know Aunt Brianna."

Oh, I know her all right.

****

"Andrew James Turner!" Brianna's shriek pierced the air. "Stop that truck right now!"

Andy slammed on the brakes, nearly pitching Jackson through the windshield. He bit back an oath as his sore knee slammed into the dashboard.

"We're toast now." Andy had the sense to put the car into park before he hunkered down in the seat like a two-year-old playing hide-and-seek. "Look at her face. She's gonna blow a gasket."

"Let me take care of this." Jackson reached over the gear shift, switched off the engine.

"Good luck. She's no fun when she's this mad."

"Tell me about it." He'd been on the receiving end of that wrath a time or two over the years...once when he'd dump-trucked her into the cold river rapids while they were tubing during their junior year of high school. She'd come up swinging—all one hundred and twenty pounds of her, soaking wet.

She strode across the grass, cheeks flaming. Jackson slid from the truck and planted himself in her path.

"Move." She pulled up in front of him and tried to zigzag her way around to Andy. She was quick, but he was quicker—years of dodging monster-sized linebackers gave him a healthy edge.

"Say please."

"I'm not joking here, Jackson." Panting, she blew a stray strand of damp hair from her forehead and planted a hand on each hip to glare at him. "What do you think you're doing?"

The scent of vanilla on her skin distracted him. He gave her a lazy grin. "Hauling mulch, just like you asked."

Her sigh spoke volumes. "Andy, get out of the truck and come over here."

He slunk from the seat, chin up. His too-long hair slid over eyes that smoldered. "What?" His voice had a biting edge, and Jackson cringed as he waited for the fireworks to start.

"Cut the tone." Brianna crossed her arms and stood her ground. "Didn't we just have a conversation about you driving—or *not* driving, I should say."

"*You* had a conversation. I just sat there and listened."

Flames danced in her eyes. "You're only twelve, Andy. What do you think would happen next if you ran into something out here while you're messing around? Another car—the building—maybe another kid?"

"I'm not messing around, and I'm not going to run into anything. There's nothing to run into. Besides, I told you Mom lets me drive all the time."

"Well, your mom's not here. I am. And I said no driving—period."

"Man, what's the big deal? I'm not even in the road. And besides, Jackson asked me to move the truck."

Her eyes left Andy long enough to bore daggers into Jackson. "Nice going."

Andy rushed to Jackson's side. He crossed his arms and bowed up to his full height. "Hey, don't get mad at him."

"I'll get mad if I want to." She folded her arms in return, gave him attitude right back. Jackson had to hand it to her. She still had the explosive spark of a firecracker. "You disobeyed me, Andy."

"I'm not sorry I did. You treat me like a two-year-old sometimes."

"I'm just trying to keep you safe and out of trouble. You're too young to understand bad things can happen when you break the rules...things that can't be undone—ever."

"Yeah, right." He dug the toe of his sneaker into the dirt and huffed. "Just because of what happened to Grandma in that car accident, you think everyone's gonna get hurt behind the wheel. Well, I'm not. And I wish you'd quit bossing me around so much. It's really getting old."

Jackson's gut twisted when tears filled Brianna's eyes.

"Enough." He stepped between them. "I was wrong to encourage you to break a rule, Andy. I wasn't thinking, and I made a mistake. Now, you're making a mistake, too, talking to Brianna like that. It's disrespectful."

"But—"

"No excuses. When you're wrong, you should admit it."

Andy scowled and shook his head so a drape of hair fell over his forehead, hiding eyes that were dark with temper. Jackson thought the kid looked a lot like he had at twelve, when anger had nearly consumed him—anger over his move to a new school, the loss of his friends and football buddies. He'd still been smoldering over his mom's death from a long and ruthless battle with breast cancer. It was tough, he knew all too well.

Andy huffed and his shoulders slumped like a balloon deflating. "Okay. I broke a rule." He cleared his throat, sounded for the world like he was choking. "I-I'm sorry, Aunt Brianna."

She swiped an eye, sniffled. "I should ground you."

"No!" His eyes widened, and he dropped the attitude like a newspaper on fire. "I mean, please don't. I'm sorry, really I am. I'll never drive again, not 'til I get my permit, at least. And then only when you say it's okay. I promise." He crossed his heart with a muddied index finger for emphasis. "Don't make me clean the bathrooms again. I'll blow chunks if I do. Besides, Jackson said he'd toss a football with me when we're done here. He's gonna show me some moves. So, can we just get back to work?"

"Yeah." Jackson watched the firm line of Brianna's mouth soften, heard her resigned intake of breath. He pushed a little harder. "Let's say we all get back to work and get this job done. The day's not getting any younger."

Behind them a mutter of voices grew. Kids had wandered from the back of the building to watch the show. In an attempt to avoid a full-blown scene worthy of a reality show highlight reel, Jackson urged, "Come on, Bri, just drop it."

Brianna threw up her hands. "Fine. Both of you grab a rake and start spreading."

****

Brianna's belly did the mamba as she watched Jackson launch a bullet spiral to Andy. He'd stripped down to a pair of athletic shorts and a faded T-shirt with the sleeves torn out. Honed muscles rippled beneath a healthy sheen of sweat at each crisp release of the ball. She tried not to remember how those powerful arms had once drawn her close and wrapped her in a loving embrace.

"You've got good hands," he called to Andy. "This time keep your eyes on the ball and get under it. Anticipate."

"Like this?" Andy made a neat catch and cradled the ball like a baby tucked beneath one arm. He sprinted across the grass to an end-zone Jackson had marked with two spare bags of mulch.

"Yeah, you're a natural, kid."

The smile that flashed across Andy's face made his dark eyes glow and Brianna's heart throb like a drum. The sulky smirk had left him, and he looked like a carefree twelve-year-old.

Now, if we can just do something with that hair.

"Here, let me show you something." Jackson loped over, his limp a bit more pronounced than it had been at the start of the day. Hauling and spreading the mulch had obviously taken its toll.

"You should rest your leg," Brianna called.

"In a minute." He placed a firm hand on each of Andy's shoulders and turned him this way, then that, guiding his stance. "You know, you'd be able to see what you're doing better if you lost some of this rock-star hair."

"You think so?"

"Sure." Jackson gathered the caramel waves into strong hands, freeing Andy's view. "See what I mean?"

Luke would be turning six.

The thought popped into Brianna's head and her breath caught. What would it have been like to have a son—raise a son—with Jackson? What if he hadn't been drafted? He'd earned a degree in business between Saturday games and grueling daily practices. What would life have been like without the glitter and notoriety of pro football—without the distraction of hours and hours of workouts and an unforgiving travel schedule?

Brianna forced the thought away. She'd never know, and it didn't matter now, anyway. Like it or not, life goes on.

And it would go on without Jackson Reed. She'd paid her date—her part of the agreement for the online auction—by coming here today with him. They'd negotiated the details and the deal was sealed, the money safely deposited in the Thursday's Child account at the local bank.

And now it was time to leave. "Andy, we need to go."

He caught the clean spiral Jackson tossed, ran with it. He had some serious speed. "In a minute."

"Now." She sighed and propped a hand on one hip. "You've got homework, remember?"

"Yeah." He rolled his eyes. "How could I forget?"

Jackson hop-limped to Andy's side and nudged him before leaning over to whisper, "Yes, ma'am goes a long way."

"Huh?" Andy pushed sweaty hair from his eyes and cradled the football like he'd never let go.

"The r-word—respect—goes a long way."

“Oh, yeah.” Reluctantly, he tossed the ball to Jackson. “I guess I’d better go. Thanks for throwing with me. It was awesome.”

“My pleasure.” Jackson tossed the ball back. “You can keep it. We’ll run a few plays again soon.”

“You mean it?”

“Wouldn’t say it if I didn’t.” He flashed a smile and wiped sweat from his face with the hem of his soiled T-shirt. The odor of mulch lingered like a second skin. “Just get the homework done and stay ungrounded. Remember...respect.”

“Got it.” Andy lobbed the ball in the air, caught it neatly as he turned to Brianna. “Yes, ma’am. I’m coming. Do we have time to go for a haircut?”

A battle waged in the pit of Brianna’s belly. Time with Jackson, his attention and help, was just what Andy needed.

And exactly what I don’t.

5

JACKSON GRIMACED AS HE PLOPPED the bag of frozen peas over his swollen knee. He'd made it through a full workout with a local trainer this morning—no painkillers, either—and that showed some progress, at least. But he was paying for it now. His knee throbbed like a knife jabbed into the tender flesh.

I won't down a painkiller...I won't.

He reached for the remote, flipped through the channels to find ESPN, and went stone cold. That dark-haired kid from the University of Florida—the one touted by every analyst across the country as the next big thing—gripped a microphone and fielded questions like he was already a seasoned pro.

And he wore a Jaguars jersey and a ball cap tugged low over smiling eyes. What was up with that? *He*—Jackson Reed—was the Jaguar's star quarterback. Had been for going on seven years. Sure, this knee injury had set him back—knocked him out of early spring practice and the first few games of the upcoming season, maybe—but he'd get his game back...eventually.

He'd dedicated his entire pro career to the Jags, given them two-hundred percent. Now this new kid, young and fresh and *glowing* with the prospect of playing in the NFL—on *his* Jaguar team, no less—drew the crowd's undivided attention.

Jackson's cell phone rang. He reached for it, glanced at the caller ID, and immediately jabbed the talk button.

"Stan, what's going on here?" He fought to keep his voice level as he spoke with his agent. "I have a little knee surgery, miss a few spring practices, and you let the team call in a new recruit?"

"Now, look, Jack," Stan's voice was thick with false bravado. "Calm down. We're just in the planning stages here. The coach said he'll give the kid a year, see what happens. No one's trying to force you out."

"So that's the way it goes, huh? I give my blood, sweat and tears for six years, Stan. *Six years*. Then one little injury and the coach turns tail on me and recruits some hotshot kid. He can't be a day over twenty-two."

"You were barely a day over twenty-two when you signed on to play, remember?"

"Of course I remember." The day was burned into his memory—the celebration when his name was called during first round draft coverage and he donned an official Jaguar's jersey and ball cap. But even then, something had been missing...

Brianna, back in Knoxville.

Her absence had left a gaping hole no amount of excitement could fill.

"The doc said—"

"I don't care what the doc said. My knee's getting better. You know me, Stan. I'm no quitter. I'll do whatever it takes to get back to playing one-hundred percent."

"I know, Jack. But this comes from the top." He paused, cleared his throat, and when he spoke again his voice was low, hushed, as if he didn't want others nearby to hear. Jackson could picture the manager and possibly even the owner standing just outside the office door, ears trained on the conversation. "Football is about money, Jackson. People don't want to pay big bucks for a product that can't deliver. And, after it's all said and done, that's what it boils down to, Jack—you're a product. But we'll find a way around this, even if you *do* have to ride the bench for a while. Your endorsements are strong and that carries some weight. As a matter of fact—"

"Hold up a minute." Jackson crushed the soda can he held. Dark, syrupy liquid splattered the coffee table. "What did you say? I'm a *what*?"

"You heard me—a product. That's the reality of it. I'm sorry, Jack, but this kid from Florida is the real deal. Through his college career he's built a fan base that's unbelievable, and we all know what that means."

"Yeah, I know—cold, hard cash for the team's coffers. Well, I have a fan base, too. At least, I *thought* I had a fan base. And I've made more than my fair share of money for you, as well. Have you forgotten that so quickly, Stan? Have you forgotten I led the team to the playoffs just a few months ago, and that lined your pockets with a healthy wad of green?"

"Nobody's forgotten anything." Another pause followed a heavy, dramatic sigh which signaled that, like it or not, the conversation was coming to an end. "Look, Jack, this call's as hard for me as it is for you—"

Yeah, right.

"Just continue to do what the doc says, and don't sweat it too much. Work out like it's a matter of life or death, get the strength and speed back. Then we'll see how things go...okay?"

"Sure, Stan...then we'll see."

He jabbed the end button, tossed the phone onto the polished wood floor and felt like stomping it into a million pieces. Instead, he reached for the familiar amber bottle of painkillers. His hands shook as he popped the lid and tossed one of the colorful capsules into his mouth. Before he could swallow, though, bitterness soured his tongue and he spit the capsule out. He couldn't breathe, couldn't think. The whole world seemed to go black.

Apparently, he was washed up at the ripe old age of twenty-nine—at least with the team he thought would stand by him. No way he'd ride the bench, play second fiddle to some kid green out of college. He hung his head, thought he might hyperventilate right there in the living room, in front of the flat-screen TV with a turkey-on-wheat sandwich propped in his lap and a bag of frozen vegetables slung cold across one knee.

Get a grip, Jackson. Get a grip.

He held his head in his hands and was surprised when the jumbled thoughts that swam through his brain merged into a furtive prayer.

Dear God, help me. I don't know what to do.

He didn't pray to play football again...he didn't pray for more money, more fame. No, he asked for guidance and to be shown the way he should go. Because where he was sitting right now felt bad...the worst. And there appeared to be no light on the horizon. Not even a glimmer.

So he bowed his head and prayed some more. And a gentle peace washed over him.

****

Brianna found Jackson at the side of the building, in the place where afternoon sunlight was most brilliant...the place where she'd dreamed of a vegetable garden for the kids.

It was a good skill to have—gardening. There was little in life more satisfying than planting a seed and nurturing it, watching it grow strong and vibrant. Her mom had introduced her to the joys of gardening when she was very young. Together, they'd created a small indoor greenhouse beneath a brilliant ray of sunlight that streamed through their enclosed back porch, when a whisper of cold still chilled the late-winter air. Then, they'd replanted the seedlings into a plot her dad tilled rich and smooth. The scent of fertile earth mixed with musky compost was like an old friend. It became a family tradition—planting a garden together, tending it and watching it grow.

Until the Saturday her mom died in a car accident, rushing home from the grocery store with Terri at the wheel. It happened on a warm, impossibly clear day the late-spring of her freshman year of high school, on an afternoon filled with sunshine that held the promise nothing bad could ever happen in the world.

She'd been hanging out at the quarry with Jackson, where they swam for hours beneath shimmery sunlight that felt like it belonged to mid-July. And he'd bought her a fudge-dipped soft-serve cone that melted faster than she could eat it. She'd giggled as the sticky mess dripped down her chin and splattered across the new coral-colored flip-flops Mom had surprised her with just that morning.

And when they returned home, exhausted and kissed by the sun, her dad was there in the living room waiting with Jackson's dad. One glance at their grief-stricken, red-rimmed eyes and she knew something awful had happened...somehow she knew without a word being spoken. Days of darkness followed, and her world felt suffocating, like a musty room with no windows.

When her mom died, the gardens had died away, too, and her dad sold the house the summer she graduated. She drove by the brick rancher once in a while on her way home from work just to look, to remember, and found the beloved plot of land along the back fence covered with weeds.

But this spring a desire rose in Brianna. She had Thursday's Child to nurture and grow, and what a way to honor her mom's memory...teaching the kids to stake tomato plants and trellis cucumbers, sprinkle fertilizer and watch plump, round pumpkins turn from deep green to vibrant orange, as her mom had once taught her.

She'd like to eventually build a greenhouse, too, and perhaps show the kids how to cultivate a variety of colorful spring flowers and crisp summer vegetables to fund some of their programs. She made a mental note to discuss the idea with Renee. They might need a vendor's license or a permit of some sort. And they'd have to figure out where start-up money would come from. Renee would look into it. She was good with things like that. She'd find a way to make it happen.

Jackson's found the perfect spot.

His grunt yanked her back to the present. She loped over and stood at the edge of the plot to watch him separate stubborn patches of grass from the soil with a shovel. His jaw was set in a tight line and sweat puddled in a dark furrow of hair that gathered along the nape of his neck.

"What are you doing?"

He tossed her a glance, eyes dark and shadowed as if he hadn't had a decent night's sleep in ages. "Digging a garden."

"I see that. I mean, what are you doing *here*? How did you know I wanted a garden in this exact spot—the most perfect spot on the entire property?"

"Andy mentioned it. Said you told him over pizza one night how you'd like to make a garden for the kids someday." He lifted another square of sod, threw it onto a growing heap. "And I got to thinking...I remember your mom, Brianna, and how much it hurt you when she died that spring. You haven't picked up a hoe, watered a seedling since she was laid to rest, have you?"

Her throat tightened. Following the accident the darkness eventually lifted, but she and her dad had never mentioned gardening again. Somehow it just wouldn't have been the same. They both understood that. And Terri had refused to wander anywhere near that area of the back yard. "You're going to hurt your knee again."

"Forget about my knee." He lifted the last square of sod and dumped it onto the heap, then tossed the shovel aside. Reaching into the bed of his truck, he found a water bottle. Ice clinked along the insulated metal sides as he dipped his face toward the blazing sun and guzzled a long swig, then drenched his sweaty head with what was left. Hair dripping, he stripped off the soiled shirt, wiped his face with it, and found a clean shirt in the duffel bag he'd crammed behind the driver's seat.

He tossed the soiled shirt behind the seat and turned to her. "Get in."

"What?" Her heart did a little flip when his muscles flexed as he shimmied into the clean T-shirt. "Where are we going?"

"To the home improvement store—to get a tiller, some compost and maybe even some plants, if they have a decent selection and you feel like sorting through them."

"There's not money in our budget for a tiller, or for anything else of a gardening nature. We can't just go out and buy stuff. I have to run it by Renee, first. She manages the books...and the purse strings for Thursday's Child."

"Did I say anything about money—or a budget?"

"No, but..."

"Then just get in."

"Okay. I'm going." She eased around to the passenger side, climbed into the truck, and shook when he slammed the door hard enough to break the window glass. "What's going on, Jackson? What are you so worked up about? You look like you just lost your best friend."

He jammed the keys into the ignition and cranked the engine. His gaze locked with hers, and she found resentment there...and grief. "I do, huh?" He laughed bitterly. "I guess that makes you happy."

"Happy?" Her stomach soured at the bitterness in his voice. "How can you say such a thing?"

"Because you act like I'm a pariah. Look at the way you're clutching the door, ready to leap at any moment."

She glanced over, released the door handle, and felt her fingers tingle as blood resumed its flow. "Sorry...I'm just—I don't understand what's going on here, Jack. Is your dad okay? Did something happen?" She'd read in the newspaper he was having some heart trouble. The reporters wrote about how Jackson had flown between games last fall to stay with him through bypass surgery and recovery. Maybe there were complications.

"Dad's doing fine. The cardiologist said he's near one hundred percent again. He should live to see his great-grandchildren."

Great grandchildren...

She stiffened in the seat and splayed a hand across the dash as the truck stumbled over a pothole. "Then what's bothering you?"

"Why does something have to be bothering me? I'm digging you a garden. We're going to the home improvement store for a tiller and whatever else we need to finish the job. That's it."

"I know you better than that, Jackson. At least I used to...before..."

"Before what?"

"Nothing. Forget it. Just slow down and watch the road, would you? You're driving way too fast."

He laughed, but eased off the gas. "Some things never change, Bri."

"Really? Jack, I've been wondering…" She searched for the right words. "What it's like to…"

"To what? Just spit it out." He fumbled with the radio dials until soft music filled an awkward silence. "

Brianna picked at a piece of lint that clung to her skirt.

"What does it feel like to walk into a store and buy whatever you want without any thought about the cost—no worries about breaking the old bank account?"

"It's just…life." He shrugged. "I see what I want—what I need— and I get it. The bill comes, and I pay it."

"No sweat, right? No worries about what tomorrow might bring."

"That's your take on it, huh?" His eyes narrowed and his tone held a sharp edge. "Sure. Whatever you say...no worries." He reached for a stick of gum from a package on the console, unwrapped it and popped it into his mouth. The scent of cherries filled the car, wafted over the odor of sweaty T-shirts and musty remnants of the mulch he'd hauled a few days ago. "Any other questions?"

A million, at least. But she held her tongue. "Let's get the tiller and the other things you mentioned. We have to make this quick. I have a budget meeting with Renee in an hour that I can't miss, because when it comes to Thursday's Child the worries are endless."

He reached for her hand, gave her fingers a gentle squeeze before skimming his thumb along her ring finger where the token of his love and his promise had once sat.

His broken promise.

"I'm sorry, Bri." Jackson's voice invaded her thoughts, his tone suddenly gentle. "Let me shoulder those worries for a little while. Relax and enjoy the ride. I'll get you back for your meeting with time to spare."

****

"This can't be right." Brianna's eyes grazed the paper once more, searching for an error in calculations.

"It's dead right." Renee frowned. "I was up half the night crunching and re-crunching numbers. There's no mistake, Bri. Thursday's Child is in a world of hurt."

"But what about the auction? That brought in what—fifty thousand? Shouldn't that cover us for a while?"

"You know the rent on this building and the grounds alone comes to five figures each month. Then there are utilities and equipment to consider, not to mention the extra staff we'll have to hire for the summer, as well as insurance and taxes."

"We can cut our salaries. I don't need much to live on."

"You already took a pay cut a few months ago, and that was before Andy came to live with you. Think of him, Brianna. The kid eats what's left of your salary in food alone each month. You can't whittle any more than you already have."

She sighed, paced the floor. "This is our dream, Renee. We've worked so hard, and the kids need us. We can't let them down. We just have to hang on a little longer. Something will happen. I just know it will."

"Yeah. The doors are gonna get padlocked when we can't make the rent."

"Don't say that." She gnawed her lower lip. "We'll make it."

"Even if we do, you know the building's going up for sale come August. Then what, Brianna? Even though we have first rights for purchase, you know we can't afford to buy it. Where are we going to go?"

"There's got to be a way. Have faith, Renee. If we go down, it won't be without a fight. Your idea to have the silent auction was a good one. It brought in a substantial chunk of money—"

"Thanks to Jackson."

"Maybe so. I'll admit he was more than generous. But we have to come up with additional ideas to raise funds. Let's put our thinking caps on and work through this. I'll get some paper, take a few notes."

"Okay," Renee agreed. "But we'd better order in a pizza. I have a feeling it's gonna be another late night."

****

Female voices drifted down the hall. Jackson recognized Brianna's melodic southern cadence, and assumed the second belonged to Renee. They were deep in discussion, tossing ideas back and forth.

"We can't quit now." Brianna's voice quickened with urgency. "Come on, Renee. You're the financial wizard here. Think...think."

"I *am* thinking, Bri. Calm down. Here, have a handful of trail mix. You know how cranky you get when your blood sugar drops."

"I do *not* get cranky."

"Yeah, right. Eat the trail mix."

Jackson swiped a forearm across his brow. Sweat ran down his back and soaked his dirt-splattered T-shirt, but the garden was ready. He glanced at his watch. The school day was nearly over. Soon the building would come to life and kids would swarm him like bees on a honeycomb. He debated...knock on the office door and interrupt Brianna's conversation or slip away quietly, before he was mauled by kids? His knee throbbed from wrestling with the tiller, and he didn't think he could gun a spiral worth a hill of beans until he rested a bit.

And I sure don't want to disappoint the kids when I'm not able to play a decent game of football with them.

"If we don't come up with something quick, we'll lose everything." Brianna's voice stopped him in his tracks. "I can't bear the thought of that, Renee. I just can't."

He leaned against the wall to take the pressure off his knee and listened to her voice rise with worry.

"What will happen to the kids?"

Jackson grimaced. I have to do something...It's killing me to hear her so torn up.

He turned an ear toward the doorway, and the sound of Brianna's voice nearly melted him. "Let's go over things again, Renee. Come on, we'll make a list."

I'll formulate a strategy, too, then make a few calls of my own when I get home.

6

BRIANNA SMILED AS A CROWD of kids tackled Jackson in the field behind the Thursday's Child the next week. He fell into the grass and made a grand production of splaying his arms and acting like they'd knocked him out cold. When they poked and prodded like ants swarming a hill, his eyes flew wide and he rose up with a roar to chase them.

His limp's almost gone. He'll probably be gone soon, too.

Brianna drove around the parking lot to a space near the action and shut off the car's engine. A dull thud of tension drummed across her forehead, and she pinched the bridge of her nose to stave it off.

Andy was in trouble again. Well...kind of in trouble. His math teacher had called because some sort of project was due—apparently had been due—for a week now and Andy had yet to turn it in. Most teachers would have given him an F and moved on, but not Mr. Grinstead. No, Andy would do the project *and* be assigned eternal detention, as well. He might stay in detention until he was old enough to collect Social Security.

And there was no football practice in detention, sorry to say.

So Andy's only option was to turn in the project soon—like, tomorrow—and beg for leniency. And another late night poring over books at the kitchen table, listening to him moan and groan, wasn't exactly what she had on the agenda.

Brianna slid from the driver's seat and made her way toward the crowd. Something sailed through the air, and it took only a moment to determine the flying object was a football—and that Jackson delivered the sweet spiral.

"Heads up!" Jackson's voice rang across the field. A moment later the ball landed at her feet with an annoying *thump,* nearly bruising her toes. She jumped back and the throbbing in her head cranked up a notch. His voice found its way through the achy fog. "Nice catch, Bri—not."

"You could give a girl a little warning." She bent to retrieve the ball. It was the real deal...official NFL issue. No department store knockoff for Jackson Reed. "What are you doing here, Jack?"

"I came to check on the garden. Andy and I set up a sprinkler system to keep the plants watered, then he asked me to toss the ball. So, here I am. The garden looks good, by the way. Tomatoes are coming in nicely and the sprinklers should help when the hot sun of full-blown summer kicks in. No weeds, I noticed. The kids have done a good job in that department."

"Yes, they have. And I've got a stack of cards in my office that they made for you. They all want to thank you for your generosity. I told them you donated the tiller and the plants, dug the garden yourself. They appreciate it, Jackson—we all do."

"Want to toss the ball with us?" He eyed her linen pants and sandals that showed off the cotton-candy pink polish on her nails. "Not exactly football gear, but Andy and I will go easy on you."

"Sounds like fun but...well, I'm sorry to report Andy's done tossing the ball for the day, the week...maybe the rest of his natural life."

"What do you mean?" Andy stalked across the lawn, hands jammed into the pockets of his cargo shorts. His eyes, no longer hidden beneath a curtain of hair since Jackson suggested the cut, narrowed into a battle line. "What did I do now?"

She leveled him a look. "It's not what you did, buddy. It's what you didn't do."

He frowned. "The science fair project? It's not due for another week, and I'm working on that with Brody. We have things totally under control."

"Uh-uh. Try again."

He scratched his head a moment, then snapped his fingers. "Oh, yeah, that book report for English. But I still have—" He glanced at his watch. "—

sixteen and a half hours till it's due. That's plenty of time to get things done. I only have two more chapters to read, and the epilogue. What's the rush?"

Not a book report, too. Will summer, and freedom from this schoolwork, ever arrive?

Brianna groaned. She felt her pulse quicken to a dangerous speed. "Strike two. Does math ring a bell...a math *project*? Perhaps something important that was due, say, last week. Last Tuesday, to be exact."

"Oh, that, yeah. I...guess I forgot about it. I should have made a note in my planner, but..." He had the sense to lower his head, slap on a repentant look. "How did you know?"

She pulled out her cell phone, waggled it in front of his face. "Mr. Grinstead just called. Isn't technology wonderful?"

"Nope." He grimaced. "I'd have to disagree, totally."

"Despite that opinion…" She handed him the football. "Give it back to Jackson. You're done with the game for a while."

His eyes flew wide with disappointment. "But—"

"Don't even try to argue. A math project *and* a book report? And you haven't even finished the book yet? Your procrastination's giving me heart palpitations, Andy. My hair's going gray, and fast."

"It doesn't look gray to me," Jackson chimed in. "Looks good, shiny...sassy."

She shot daggers in his direction. "You stay out of this."

He raised both hands, palms facing her. "I'm innocent.

"Yeah, right." She turned back to Andy. "Get whatever you need and march straight to my office—no detours. Get started on that project—and the book report."

He dug the toe of his tennis shoe into the grass. "Geez, why do I have to go to school? I'm gonna be a pro football player. I don't need an education. I'll make a ton of money without one." He tossed Jackson the ball. "Magazines will be hounding me for interviews, and maybe I'll even get paid to be on the cover of Sports Illustrated. You got to do that, didn't you, Jackson? Tell her."

Jackson went stone still. His gaze locked with Brianna's, and when she opened her mouth to give Andy what-for he shook his head ever so slightly and murmured, "Let me handle this."

"Jackson—"

"I've got it under control. I'll take Andy in, help him get started. You just take care of whatever needs taking care of around here, okay? Renee was looking for you earlier—something about the budget."

Oh, the budget...

"But—"

Jackson shook his head again. His eyes were pleading. "Give it a rest, Bri. I've got this one."

She sighed. The pain in her head made the world around her go gray. She didn't have the energy to battle. Not now, not here—not like this. "Oh, all right. But make sure he gets right to work, or we'll be up all night. And I need some sleep tonight...I really need some sleep."

"Oh, don't worry. I'll make sure he gets everything done." He slung an arm over Andy's shoulder and tossed the ball back to a kid behind him. "You guys carry on with the game. I'll be back in a while."

Brianna sighed as grumbling erupted. "No fair," Caleb groaned. A shock of red hair glowed like flames beneath bright sunlight, and freckles spattered his pale cheeks. "Why does Jackson have to quit just because Andy has homework? I still wanna throw."

"Me, too," Alex joined in.

"Yeah, me too." Their voices washed over one another until all that remained was a cacophonous storm.

Brianna held up a hand to silence the chaos. "Jackson said he'll come back soon," she assured the group that threatened to turn into a mob. "Why don't you toss the ball around, practice your game while you wait? Maybe you can show him some new moves when he gets back."

"Good idea," Anna, the dark-haired girl who'd joined them just a few weeks ago, agreed. "We'll run a few plays, show him what we can do."

"He'll be impressed, I'm sure," Brianna encouraged. "I'll watch for a few minutes, see what you've got."

Maybe, with any luck, I'll coax this headache from a ferocious roar to a mild purr in the meantime.

"You know about football?" Caleb asked, his eyes narrow with skepticism.

"Sure. I used to watch it all the time." She'd been Jackson's biggest fan, front and center at every game. She'd learned how to massage his sore muscles and feed his voracious appetite during two-a-day—sometimes even three-a-day—training sessions. She'd listened to him lament over every loss, every fumble and interception, every bad call, and celebrated sweet victories with him, as well.

"But I've never heard you talk about it," Anna continued. "How come? Miss Renee goes to all the home football games and Mr. Branson likes to watch them on TV, but you've never mentioned football."

"I don't watch it anymore. At least I haven't lately. I've been very busy. There's a lot to do around here, and it takes up most of my time." She grinned, though the effort nearly split her head wide open. "You guys keep me hopping."

"Maybe Jackson can help get you interested in it again. He's sure a good player, isn't he? Too bad his knee hurts." Anna brightened, and her smile revealed two shiny metallic rows of braces bound by navy blue and canary-yellow bands...her school colors. "It's getting better, though. He said so."

"Yes, I hope so." It would get better, and he'd go back to practice again with the NFL. Actually, spring training had already begun.

Why isn't he in Jacksonville?

She tossed the ball to Caleb. "Go run some plays now. I'll watch."

"Okay, Miss Brianna. Here we go."

She enjoyed the warm sunshine on her face, the sound of laughter and easy banter that filled the air. She breathed in the sweet scent of lilac bushes Jackson had helped plant last weekend, and forgot about the dire financial straits of Thursday's Child and Andy's mound of homework. Soon the headache eased to a dull throb, then fled altogether.

****

"You really have a degree in business?" Andy's eyes flew wide. He'd dumped the contents of his backpack onto Brianna's desk and sorted the stuff into two piles—what he needed...notebook, math book, pencil. And what he didn't...IPod, sketch pad, wadded up notes he and Brody had passed during English class. Jackson watched, remembering the heaps of notes he'd sneaked to Brianna during their classes together.

He still had a few, tucked neatly between the yellowed pages of his high school yearbooks. Every once in a while he took them out, smoothed the crinkled paper, read them...and remembered. “But I thought you played football when you were in college.”

“I did play football, but I had to go to class, too.” He reached for Andy’s math book and scanned the lesson waiting to be completed. “You can’t just go to college to play sports. You have to work toward a degree and keep your grades up. I chose to study business and marketing.”

“But, why? You’re never gonna use it, are you?”

“Sure. I’ve already used it. Football has a business side, you know.”

“How so?”

That’s what it boils down to, Jack...you’re a product.

Jackson stuffed the thought and was careful to keep his tone light. “It’s not just all about throwing the ball and running plays.” He shrugged. “Besides, my body won’t hold out forever. Then, what? It’s good to have something to fall back on.”

“But don’t football players make a ton of money?”

“That depends.”

“You have, though. Right?

“I’ve done okay.”

The kid had stars in his eyes, and Jackson wondered if he'd looked the same when he was
young and dreamed of making it big. "But there are no guarantees."

"I don't get it." Andy doodled across a scrap of paper. "If you spend time studying in college you have less time to practice. And if you have less time to practice, you might not get recruited to go pro, right?"

"And if you don't study, don't make the grades through high school, no college will even consider looking at you—or keeping you, so there's no chance at all of being recruited. You have to have the whole package, sport—brains, talent, and a whole lot of hard work."

"Oh, then forget it."

"What? You have an aversion to hard work?"

"No. It's not that. It's just...my grades aren't the best."

"And why is that? You seem smart enough to me—or do you just put on a good show?"

"Aunt Brianna says I'm smart, but I don't apply myself."

"I'd have to agree with her on this one."

"But I'll never get all this work done. And even if I do, I'm gonna fail math anyway. Mr. Grinstead hates me."

"Hate's a strong word. Mr. Grinstead's tough. I know from personal experience. But I can't imagine him hating anyone—not even Billy Huggins, who put a night crawler in his coffee."

"He did? When?"

"Before your time, sport. Old Grinstead took a huge gulp from his mug, choked on the wiggly thing. He was up in front of the class, gagging and turning every color of the rainbow. I sprang from my seat to give him the Heimlich. We'd just learned how to do that in our first aide class, and I'd paid attention." He laughed, remembering. "I was teacher's pet after that, no denying it. Saved the old man's life, I did."

"Wow. That's cool. What happened to Billy Huggins?"

"No one knows for sure. He was sent home and never came back. One thing's for certain, though—he didn't play in the NFL"

"Well, since Mr. Grinstead likes you so much, maybe you can put in a good word for me, get him off my back. Maybe he'll forget about the math project...and detention."

"No dice. I'll put in a good word—maybe—but you're going to do the project. I promised Brianna you'd get it done, so let's get started."

"Aw, I thought you were on my side."

"I am. That's why you're going to do every bit of it. Now, where's the outline. I'll show you a shortcut."

Andy flipped open his math book. "A shortcut. Cool."

****

"He's really finished with everything?" Brianna leaned against the door jamb and studied Jackson, who relaxed in her rolling desk chair, his feet propped neatly on the cluttered desktop.

"Yes, really." He winked, and his dark eyes drew her in. "I do have a miracle or two tucked up my sleeve."

"Thanks, Jackson." She tore open a package of cashews and offered him some before tossing a handful into her mouth. The salt soothed her taste buds as her belly rumbled. "I appreciate your help. I didn't mean to stay outside so long."

"The kids roped you into playing a scrimmage or two. I saw you run a few plays through the window." He grinned. "I forgot how quick you can move."

"Luckily I had a pair of running shoes in the car. I would have never made it in these sandals." She sighed. "It was fun. I used to play with the kids all the time, but I've had more paperwork lately, more planning sessions. That takes time away from the action. I miss it, but I guess I haven't lost all my moves. I only got tackled a few times, anyway."

"No broken bones, so it hardly counts."

"Guess not." Brianna gathered the papers on her desk into a pile and slipped an array of pens into a ceramic jar. The center had closed half an hour ago, and Andy was busy shooting baskets in the gym to work off some energy. Down the hallway, she heard the hard slap of rubber against polished wood. "Sometimes the responsibility is overwhelming. Andy is a lot of work, but a lot of fun, too."

"How'd he come to...um...live with you?"

"It's a long story."

"I've got time."

Hunger gnawed at her belly and she felt the lure of a long, hot shower, but she knew if she left without giving Andy time to work out the unbridled energy raging in his system she'd just pay for it later, when she had to fight with him to go to bed. So she gave up on organizing and took a seat on the edge of the desk.

"Well...when my dad died he didn't have much to show for a lifetime of hard work, but what he did have he left to Terri and me, equally. We sold the house, and I used my part of the money to open this place. Terri decided she wanted to be an actress, so she moved to Los Angeles. She spent two years there, hunting down auditions and networking with agents and people who said they knew a thing or two about the business. And that was hard enough on Andy, since he was left alone most nights. Anyway, it didn't work out, and she got mixed up with a bad crowd, blew through most of her savings. So, she decided maybe fashion is her thing. She's in New York looking for work, last I heard."

"I'm sorry, Bri. I didn't know."

"How could you?" Her voice didn't accuse, just stated the facts. "She had a harder time than me, Jackson. The guilt's eaten away at her."

"It shouldn't. She was only seventeen when she...when your mom..."

"I know. But she doesn't see it that way. She feels responsible." She slipped her sandals off, pressed the soles of her feet against cool tile. "Anyway, when she decided to move to New York Andy was dead-set against going. He ran away—twice. So I offered to take him in. He wasn't real thrilled with that option, either, but it was better than long nights left home all alone in New York. I guess he'd had enough of that in California. Needless to say, it's been...interesting."

"I can only imagine."

"He's a great kid, really. He's just lacking some boundaries, and he's a little bit insecure."

"That's understandable." Jackson reached into his pocket for a pack of gum and offered her a stick. She unwrapped it and the scent of cherries filled the air. "He asked me if we used to date."

"What? Why?" She gagged on the wad of gum she'd pressed into her mouth and Jackson sprang from the chair to smack her soundly between the shoulder blades.

"You okay?"

She nodded as she wiped tears from her eyes and coughed to clear the rock from her throat. "I-I think so. How did he know...about us?"

"He found a photo of us together, dressed in formal-wear. Apparently, it fell out of one of the paperbacks you loaned him."

"Oh, that must have been homecoming...senior year." Unable to bring herself to destroy the photo after Jackson left, she'd slipped it between pages of the book and forgotten it.

He leaned back against the wall and jammed his hands into the pockets of his jeans. "I remember how beautiful you looked. Man, you stopped my heart that night when you floated down the stairs in that silver-sequined dress, the strappy sandals...wow."

She was surprised he remembered. She'd loved that dress...felt like a princess in it. *He'd* made her feel like a princess. "That was a long time ago, Jackson. A lifetime ago."

"Seems like just yesterday. Remember how we made a pact to go as friends, because college was looming in the distance and we didn't know for sure where we'd be...didn't want to have a hard goodbye? And then at the lake afterwards, beneath the light of a full moon, you let me kiss you?"

She shivered at the thought. It had been completely unplanned, unexpected. His body was warm, protective as he gently eased her against him. And the kiss...he'd smelled of cherries and woodsy aftershave, just like he did now. Oh, how his strength caused a tingle to race from the top of her head to the pit of her belly. He'd kissed the breath right out of her and it was simply...amazing.

She worked the gum, fought to clear the memory from her mind. "I'd rather not talk about it." It had been the bridge between their friendship and a newfound romance, a bond that went deeper than friends skipping rocks down at the pond or doing homework together over a plate of warm chocolate chip cookies. And through it all, Jackson had been wonderful...patient and loving—until the lure of wealth and fame changed him. Brianna wound a strand of blonde hair around her index finger and changed the subject—fast. "Um, Andy seems to like you."

His gaze held hers, and he was quiet a moment. He slid a second stick of gum into his mouth and worked the gooey mass into submission. "It's mutual. I'd like to take him to the Orange and White game this weekend, give him a taste of some real football. Maybe it will motivate him to try harder in school." He cleared his throat and his gaze pierced hers. "I'd like it, Bri, if you'd come, too."

She rushed to the desk and began to gather scraps of paper filled with scribbled notes. “Oh, Jackson, I...I don’t know. There’s so much to do here, and—”

He touched her shoulder gently and she turned back to look at him. “You don’t have to tell me now. Just think about it, okay?”

“O-okay.” She could do that much, at least.

His cell phone rang, startling them both. He answered, listened, then hung up and said, “Don’t go anywhere. I’ll be right back.”

Her stomach growled in response, and he laughed as he strode from the room to disappear down the hall.

Oh, he’s impossible!

She collapsed into the rolling chair and laid her head on the desk. Would this day ever end? She longed for the spray of a hot shower and the warmth of her down comforter.

Max must be ravenous. I’ll bet Andy forgot to feed him again this morning.

Jackson returned carrying a large white sack and a stainless steel carafe. The aroma of tangy spaghetti sauce and hazelnut coffee made her mouth water.

“Jackson, what on earth...?”

He grinned and set the sack on her desk. “They can hear your belly roaring as far as the highway. You need to eat, Bri.”

She pressed a hand to her midsection. "It's late. I should get Andy home."

"Andy's fine." The echo of a bouncing basketball proved it. Jack removed two foil pans from the sack along with plastic forks and knives. "I remember how much you like spinach ravioli from Bellacino's...and their hazelnut-vanilla latte."

"But they don't deliver. How—"

"Don't worry about how. Just fill your belly, okay?" He uncovered one of the pans and pressed it into her hands. Fat ravioli drenched in warm marinara sauce and smothered with melted mozzarella nearly brought her to tears. "Dig in. And if you're worried the coffee will keep you up all night—don't. It's decaf."

"You thought of everything, didn't you?"

"Hardly." He stuffed a forkful of pepperoni-and-mushroom calzone into his mouth and poured her a cup of latte. Steam rose and swirled, and the rich aroma made her senses sing. "But this will have to do, for now."

"Thank you."

They ate in companionable silence while the sound of Andy playing in the gym serenaded. From time to time the slap of his shoes, the thump of the ball, paused briefly and his groans over an easy missed shot reverberated up the hall.

He'll sleep well tonight, Brianna thought with a sigh of relief.

Outside the office window a full moon cast a hazy glow over the empty parking lot.

"When will you go back?" Brianna delved into a ravioli, speared a bite and drowned it in marinara before slipping it into her mouth.

"To Jacksonville?" Jackson's calzone was nearly gone. "I don't know."

"But you're going back...right?"

"I'm under contract." She heard the hesitation in his voice. "I'm obligated."

The ravioli turned to stone in her belly. She set the container on the desk. "Of course. I understand, Jackson."

His gaze found hers, held. "Do you?"

She sighed. "Does it matter?"

"Yes."

Then I don't understand any of this. Why did you come back here now...like this?

Brianna tamped down the thought. "Thanks for the food, Jackson. It was...delicious. Now, I really have to get Andy home. He'll be a bear to wake up for school tomorrow morning."

"Okay. Just one more cup of coffee for you while I clean things up here." Jackson refilled her mug as he motioned to the ravioli container, empty now except for remnants of marinara sauce. "Boy, you *were* hungry."

"I guess..." Now she wished she hadn't polished off every bit of the food. Her twisted belly was already revolting. "I didn't realize."

He took the container from her, stuffed it into the delivery bag along with his. "I'll take this, throw it away. The custodian's already been through your office. I don't want to leave a mess when she's worked so hard to make things look good."

Brianna gaped. He sounded like the old Jackson, the one who took extra time to care about people, even the people most others deemed insignificant.

"Yes, Rhonda's a hardworking employee who has a heart for the kids. I know she'll appreciate the thoughtfulness, Jackson. Thank you."

"You're welcome." He stood, cleared his throat. "I'll go down to the gym and tell Andy to head this way. Then I guess I'll...see you tomorrow."

"Tomorrow?"

"Here, at the center. I told the kids I'd toss the ball around again. They seem to like it well enough."

"Oh, Jack, you don't have to. Your knee's not completely healed. I'd hate for you to damage it again."

"Forget about my knee." A shadow crossed his eyes. Was that doubt she saw? No, it couldn't be. Jackson never doubted anything. Once he made a decision he went with it...no looking back. He'd probably never so much as given her a second thought after he walked out that long-ago night. The headlines screamed of his wild adventures with other women. Even if only a fraction of the stories were true...well, she just couldn't stomach the thought. No, Jackson hadn't been lonely, or plagued with grief over the end of their relationship. He'd gone on, made his pocketful of money, enjoyed his fame—no strings attached. "You just...take care of the kids and business here. I'll handle the rest."

That's what worries me...the rest.

7

DOUBT STABBED AT JACKSON, TWISTED like a knife plunged into his gut. He barely heard the steady hum of traffic that flowed down Kingston Pike past the open-air café where he sat beneath a colorful umbrella meant to chase the heat of the sun away. What had he been thinking, to walk out on Brianna the way he did? She was the best thing that ever happened to him.

"Jackson...earth to Jackson." His dad's voice broke into his thoughts. "Where are you, Jack?"

"Sorry." He forced his eyes to focus on the glass of sweet tea that sat on the table in front of him. He reached for it, drew a long, cool swig as condensation from the glass slicked his hand. "I'm listening."

"No, you're not." His dad's deep blue eyes were filled with concern. "You're worlds away, son. What's on your mind?"

"It's just...a lot is up in the air right now with my playing time. This new kid from Jacksonville's really thrown a wrench into the mix. Seems he's an overnight sensation, and I don't know, given this knee, just where that leaves me."

"Nobody's an overnight sensation, Jack. You know that better than anyone. It takes years of practice, sweat, and sacrifice, especially to get to this level. The kid has talent, sure. But if you take a look at his history, it shows a great deal of hard work, as well."

Jackson sighed. When Dad put it like that, well, it made him ashamed of his quick judgment. "I guess you're right."

"What do you want, son?"

"I...don't know."

"You know I don't like to mince words, so I'm going to come right out with this." Dad sighed heavily. "Jackson, do you still love the game?"

The question startled him, and his gut clenched, churning the burger he'd just devoured. He lowered his gaze. "Yes. I mean...I don't know anymore. Maybe not...as much."

"Well, then, that presents a problem. You know from the start I told you—"

"I know—love of the game comes first, and the rest will all fall into place."

"That's right. So I guess you have some serious thinking to do. Better get on it—and soon."

"I-I know." That was part of the problem. Seeing Brianna again...spending time with her…jumbled his thoughts. He didn't know what he wanted anymore.

"If you still want to play, you need to get back down there with the team, get with the trainer. He'll whip your knee into shape in no time. Then things will work themselves out. You'll see. And if you don't still have the desire to play...well...I guess things will work out there, too."

Jackson drained his glass, then crumpled his napkin and tossed it on the table. "I...um...there's more, Dad."

"Of course. There always is." The concern in his eyes eased the tension in Jackson's gut down a notch. "Tell me, son."

"I'm seeing Brianna. I mean, not *seeing* her, like dating or anything, but we've spent quite a bit of time together and—"

"And you still have feelings for her?"

"Maybe...I don't know…yes. But she's so angry with me, and I guess I deserve it. I hurt her pretty bad."

"Yes, you did, Jack." Dad leaned an elbow on the table and scratched his chin. "Have you told her you're sorry?"

"Uh-uh." The admission embarrassed him. How could he have gone this long with no apology? No wonder she was angry...distant...confused.

"Well, that would be a good place to start."

"It's hard. She's got this look in her eyes when she's around me...kind of wounded, guarded. With everyone else she lights up like sunshine, but with me—no."

"Yes, Brianna always was like a luminous ray of sunshine." Dad smiled. "Her love for the Lord shines through, Jackson." His gaze leveled a challenge as his voice adopted a firm edge. "Your decisions sound more serious than I thought. Be careful, Jack. You don't want to make the same mistakes twice."

Jackson reached across the table and grasped the hand that had held his through so many challenges, so many hurts. His father's fingers were fragile now, the skin thinning and mottled with age, but the grip held firm. "Help me, Dad."

"You're asking the wrong father."

"What do you mean?"

"Have you prayed about this, Jackson?"

"Prayed? Maybe a little." He sighed heavily as his face heated with shame. "No, not enough."

Dad's gaze held tight. "That's the first step, son. Without prayer, the rest is fruitless. You should know that by now."

"But—"

"I can't help you with this, Jack." Dad released his grip, patted his hand. "You have to figure it out on your own. I'd take a knee if I were you—and soon."

****

The roar of the lawn mower greeted Brianna when she pulled up the driveway of the small, white frame house she'd purchased two years ago. The place needed some work, but it had loads of character. She loved the wrap-around porch and the tall weeping willow that shaded the front lawn like a graceful sentinel.

Max barked around back as the mower hummed. Good, Andy had started his chores without being reminded.

Now that's progress.

She shouldered a sack of groceries as she scooted from the car. Tacos—Andy's favorite—were on the menu tonight.

Her stomach felt a bit uneasy with the nagging thought that she had to call Jackson and give him her decision about going to the Orange and White game tomorrow. She'd put it off as long as possible, because she knew she couldn't—no, she shouldn't—go. What was the point? It would only serve to encourage him, and that was playing with fire. Andy didn't know it yet, but he wasn't going either. There was no point in him drawing closer to Jackson.

Because sooner or later—most likely sooner—Jackson will leave for spring training to resume his pursuit of fame and fortune.

There was no other option for him—football was in his blood. She hoped whipping up some tasty tacos would ease the sting of Andy's disappointment. He would be beyond mad, but eventually he'd realize her decision was for the best.

Yeah...in a million years, maybe.

She rounded the corner of the house to find Jackson shoving her push-mower through overgrown grass. Shock made her bobble the sack.

Across the yard, Andy wielded a weed eater, one she didn't recognize—since she didn't own a weed eater— along the outside of the fence. And to make matters worse, Max—the lug of a traitor—loped merrily at Jackson's side.

"Hey!" She plopped the sack of groceries on the tailgate of Jackson's truck and fanned her arms to get his attention. "Hey, hold up a minute."

He glanced over, grinned like he belonged there, and had the nerve to wave. Well, she'd show him. She opened the gate and ignored Max when he lunged to greet her. He danced merrily around her feet as she strode into Jackson's path and planted herself, arms crossed.

He stopped just short of mauling her freshly-painted toes. He switched off the mower and the noise level went down a few decimals, but Andy's weed eater still shrieked. "That was dangerous." His tone was matter-of-fact. "Step aside. You're in the way."

"Last time I checked, this was *my* house, *my* yard."

"So?"

"So?" She sputtered. "So, what are you doing here, mowing my lawn?"

"Helping."

"Helping? But, how did you know where I live? How did you know the lawn needed mowing? Where did that weed eater come from? And what made you think I'd want your help?"

He swiped the hem of his T-shirt across a sweat-dampened forehead and shook his head. The scent of a hard-day's work clung to his skin. "That's way too many questions for one afternoon, especially a hot one like this." He cranked the mower again and shouted over the roar of the engine. "Just go on into the house and do...well...whatever you do when you come home from a long day at work."

"I make dinner," she shouted back. "And enjoy some peace and quiet…which isn't going to happen with that mower howling."

"Dinner?" He glossed right over the peace-and-quiet point. "What's for dinner?"

Her chin came up and her arms tightened over her midsection. "Nothing for you. You can't stay."

"Mowing sure builds up an appetite." A thin sheen of sweat covered his powerful arms from his wrists to the strong curve of his shoulders. "And this grass is more like a jungle than a lawn. I don't think I can make the drive home without some sustenance. Andy said something about tacos on the menu tonight. Perfect. You know I love tacos."

"Jackson, you're impossible." She didn't know whether to laugh or cry. He was simply...exasperating. "You can't just come to my house and start mowing."

He scratched his head, tilted the brim of his ball cap forward to shade his eyes from the hot sun. "Why not?"

"It's just—it's just. Oh!" She felt like stomping her foot, throwing herself on the ground and indulging in a full-blown temper tantrum.

"You're going to make Andy feel bad. He wanted to surprise you. He said you've been working so hard lately at the center, and helping him with his homework." He leaned over, murmured. "I shouldn't let the cat out of the bag, but he's gonna tell you he made an A on that math project...*and* on the book report, too."

"He did?" To her utter displeasure, she felt her resolve begin to wear away. "Really?"

Oh, how does he manage to do that?

"Yeah, really. But when he tells you, you have to act surprised. I don't want him to know I said anything."

She pressed a hand to her mouth. "My lips are sealed."

"Good. Now, if you'll just let me finish taming this yard, I'll get back in my truck and out of your hair."

"Oh. You...you don't have to go." Suddenly she wanted him to stay and share a meal. After all, Andy was—could it really be—weed-eating the yard. And he even smiled as he sang along to music that flowed from the ear buds of the iPod he'd stuffed into his pocket.

Jackson let the mower die once more. His gaze narrowed with confusion. "Why the sudden change of heart?"

"I don't know...you took the time to help Andy, and that means a lot to me. Besides, I guess it wouldn't be very nice of me to send you home without supper after you've tamed this jungle of a lawn, especially in this heat. And you do love tacos..."

He studied her as he spoke slowly, carefully. "I don't want to make you feel uncomfortable."

"It's too late for that, Jackson." She sighed and turned to pace the swatch of lawn he'd already mowed. Blades of grass clung to her sandals. "The moment I saw you again, I felt uncomfortable."

"I'd like the discomfort to go away."

"I'd like that, too, but I don't think that's possible. I'd better go inside and get dinner started."

"Wait." He reached for her hand. His skin was callused from years of weightlifting and handling a football. His fingers, stained with grass and smelling of the gasoline that he'd poured to fuel the mower, twined with hers. He lowered his voice, and his gaze sought hers, held steady. "I'm sorry, Brianna."

For the slightest moment, her heart stopped beating. The world seemed to tilt and she stumbled back, startled by his words.

"What?"

"I'm sorry I hurt you. It was horrible, the way I treated you. Can you ever forgive me?"

Sunspots danced before her eyes, and for a moment she couldn't find her voice.

He's sorry...

"I-I have to go in the house now, Jackson. The food is going to spoil in this heat, and Andy will be ravenous soon enough."

Confusion clouded his eyes. He released her hand. "Okay."

"You can...come in when you're done. I'll have dinner waiting."

She stumbled around to the garage, taking Max with her. Up the stairs and into the kitchen, she leaned against the counter, her heart racing, head swimming, as the dog sniffed around the kitchen floor, found a suitable place beneath the table, and curled up with his head propped on his front paws.

What had just happened? Jackson had apologized—no! It wasn't fair, after all this time. What would she do with his apology, and where would she stuff the resentment, the hurt and disappointment that had become her faithful companions?

How can I forgive him?

Tears stung her eyes as she dumped the contents of the grocery sack onto the counter. She threw open a cabinet and clattered through stacks of pots and pans until she found the skillet she wanted. Soon, ground beef sizzled in the pan, and she diced juicy tomatoes and shredded crisp lettuce leaves as if her life depended on it.

*Be kind and compassionate to one another, forgiving each other...*Ephesians 4:32 whispered to her, and she felt her heart begin to relent.

Her thoughts wandered to the many times during high school that Jackson rode his bike to her house, or drove over when he was old enough to get behind the wheel, to mow the lawn. With her mom gone, her dad working long hours, and her sister off doing who knows what, the thankless task fell to her. So Jackson came, and he helped, and afterwards they shared cold lemonade and strawberries on the back porch while mocking birds chattered in the trees beyond the fence and dogs barked at the paperboy who raced down the street.

And sometimes, as their friendship deepened into something more, she let him hold her hand and they'd shared a kiss or two beneath the warm sunlight.

She tore a paper towel from the holder and wiped the streaming tears from her cheeks.

Oh, why couldn't he just stay away and leave me—and Andy—alone?

8

SHE'S CRYING.

Jackson watched, mortified, through sliding glass doors that opened into the kitchen. Tears streamed down Brianna's flushed cheeks as she stumbled over Max to set the cozy kitchen table with three plates. He remembered the wooden table that her father had crafted well—he'd spent countless hours poring over homework with Brianna when it graced her parents' kitchen. She bent down to pat the dog's head, then dabbed her eyes with a wadded tissue.

I made her cry again. The thought turned his gut inside out.

"I finished the fence." Andy loped over to stand beside him. Blades of grass blanketed his legs from ankle to knee and ear buds dangled from his shoulders. The heavy beat of a base drum filled the air. "I'll get the sides of the driveway next. Aunt Brianna will like the way it looks, all trim and neat."

"Sounds good. I'll be finished here in ten."

"Me, too." He glanced over, noticed Brianna's car in the drive. "When did she get home?"

"About twenty minutes ago. You were down by the fence, listening to your music, so you missed her. She's inside making dinner."

"Tacos, I hope. You gonna stay?"

"If she'll let me."

"Why wouldn't she?"

Oh, the innocence of youth. Jackson dismissed the question and motioned across the yard instead. "The fence looks good. You do nice work."

"Thanks. I filled all the holes Max made, too. Every time it storms, he goes temporarily insane and tries to dig his way under the fence if we're not here to let him inside. It drives Aunt Brianna crazy."

Jackson laughed at the vision of the spunky black lab digging to China. "Has he ever made a jailbreak?"

"More times than I can count. Sometimes he doesn't just dig, but he breaks through the fence, too. See all those slats we've repaired?"

Jackson nodded. Brianna always *had* been good with a hammer and nails. The thought made his blood run hot, and he wiped beads of sweat from his brow with the hem of his T-shirt.

"Anyway," Andy continued, "when Max gets out he just runs around to the front door and barks till one of us lets him in. Aunt Brianna scolds him because he tracks mud all over the floor. But then she laughs, because it *is* kind of funny."

He remembered, growing up, all the times Brianna said she wanted a dog. Her sister had been allergic, though, so that was that.

"Do you think we can toss the ball for a while after dinner?" Andy asked. "I don't have any homework tonight."

"Sure." He'd better keep moving, clear thoughts of Brianna from his head before he ran the mower over his foot, lost a toe or two in the process. "That sounds like a plan."

"I can't wait to tell Aunt Brianna about my A's. She's gonna totally freak."

Jack pushed on, yelled over his shoulder, "I wouldn't miss it for the world."

****

"That was delicious, Bri." Jackson dropped his napkin on his plate and pushed back from the table. "I haven't tasted anything so good in ages."

"That's hard for me to believe, with all the gourmet food you pro players get to sample."

"Nothing competes with a delicious home-cooked meal."

"Yeah, Aunt Brianna," Andy chimed in. "You make the best tacos."

"Glad you like them." She smiled and drew a sip of sweet tea. She wouldn't know how the tacos tasted...she'd hardly touched her meal. Her belly squirmed with a colony of night crawlers. Jackson's familiar scent—woodsy with just a hint of cherries from the gum he liked to chew—brought back feelings best forgotten. And the fact that she felt anything for him...anything at all after all these years of heartache—the pain he'd caused—confused her.

Andy's chair scraped against the tile floor. "I'll get the football, Jackson, and we can go out back."

He shook his head. "Dishes, first, sport."

"Dishes?" Andy's mouth narrowed into a thin line. Brianna knew he was used to rushing off after dinner and leaving her to clean up the mess. And, thankful for the few minutes of peace and quiet before they tangled in a battle over homework, she was usually glad to let him. Well, maybe that would change, at least for tonight.

"Your Aunt Brianna cooked, sport, so it's only fair we clean up."

"Oh...yeah." His sail deflated. "I guess."

Jackson stood, and his height seemed to fill the small room. "Grab a towel. I'll wash—you can dry and put away, since you know where it all goes."

As Brianna watched their exchange, her face heated and her nerves hummed.

When did Jackson start calling Andy 'sport', and how did the two become close enough for it to matter?

She took her tea to the front porch and slipped into a wicker chair. She eyed chipped, dull white paint that marred the railings and thought with dismay that the wood really needed a good scraping and a fresh coat of latex before the spring rains rotted it. What must Jackson think of her tiny house, with its inexpensive yet cozy furnishings, after being surrounded for so long by the lap of luxury? She lifted her chin to chase away the embarrassment.

I've worked hard for this house, and though it might not be much compared to what Jackson has, it's mine...and Andy's now.

The melody of clinking glass and running water drifted through the open window behind her. She sighed and slipped off her sandals to cross her ankles. The topic of the Orange and White game hadn't come up during dinner, to her immense relief, but she knew she couldn't avoid it much longer. After dishes and football she'd send Jackson home with a quick dismissal after informing him that she and Andy would spend tomorrow painting the front porch, not at Neyland Stadium.

She heard the telephone ring inside, and Andy's muffled voice as he answered. A few moments later his tennis shoes slapped across the living room's polished wood floor. The screen door slammed as he rushed onto the porch and planted himself in front of her.

"Brody's on the phone." The words came in a rush of excitement. "He asked if I could hang out with him tonight. His mom and dad are gonna chaperone laser tag for their youth group and they want me to come."

"Mr. Thompson?"

"Yeah. You met him at the center last week. He's the youth pastor at Shady Grove. Brody's in my science class, and he's gonna play football with me this spring."

"Yes, I remember. You guys did that science fair project together a few weeks ago—the one on salamanders." She'd had to endure a tank of them in the house...and chase after a few that made a jailbreak and took up residence in the blankets on her bed. "I suppose it's okay. What time will you be home?"

"I dunno. Not too late, I guess."

"Find out for sure, and see how much money you'll need, okay?"

"Yeah, thanks." And he was off like a shot. She heard him convey the good news to Brody, hang up the phone, then tell Jackson if they hurried with the dishes, they'd still have time to throw the ball a bit before Brody and his folks arrived.

*Jackson...*Brianna cringed. When Andy left, she'd be alone with him. Well, maybe he'd make a quick exit, too. She'd give him a firm no on the

Orange and White game and then simply break the news to Andy tomorrow, when she slipped a paint brush into his hand instead of a football.

****

"The kitchen is clean." Jackson came onto the porch and slid into the second wicker chair. He stretched long, powerful legs...legs that dodged three-hundred pound behemoths bent on tackling him and flattening him into the ground. She'd watched him go down hard more times than she could count, just to get up and shake off the pain to run again. But now...

"Thanks." She eyed the ridge of scar that ran the length of his knee. "Did it hurt?"

He gave her an odd look. "Well, I might have a slight case of dishpan hands, but I think I'll recover."

She laughed. "No. I mean, did your knee hurt when you...fell."

"When I got crushed and ripped apart? Yeah, it hurt."

"I'm sorry." In the past she'd have smoothed a finger along the bumpy ridge to massage away the pain. "And now?"

"Just a dull ache, pretty much all the time. Doc says it'll go away eventually. I just need to be patient." He sighed. "Never was my strong suit, though, being patient."

"I disagree. I've known you to be very patient...at times."

"Yeah, when I taught you to swim. Never met a girl going on thirteen who couldn't swim until I met you."

Max chased his tail in a trio of circles, sighed and curled his massive form into a ball at Jackson's feet. Jackson laughed and bent down to run a hand along his back, give him a good scratch behind the ears. Max grumbled, rolled over, and stretched his paws in the air, exposing himself for a belly scratch. The mutt had no modesty whatsoever.

"I like my feet on the ground, thank-you-very-much." Brianna gazed at the star-filled sky. The sweet scent of fresh-mowed grass danced with wild onions. "And, as I remember, your idea of 'teaching' consisted of tossing me into the pool and dunking me."

"And you came up from the water swinging. Knocked me over the head with a kickboard. Gave me a knot the size of a quarter. It hurt for three days." He held up a trio of fingers, for emphasis.

Brianna laughed. "You deserved it."

"But I taught you, didn't I? No more floundering like a drowned cat in a thunderstorm."

"Yes, you did. I'm proud to say I can hold my own in the water now, and I've completed a few triathlons along the way to prove it. But I still prefer to run."

"Yeah. Your legs are proof of that." His gaze slid up and down the length of her calf that peeked from beneath a flowing cotton skirt. "Do you think Thursday's Child might ever have a pool? You know, swimming is an important skill for kids to have."

She lowered her gaze, shrugged. "I'm not sure Thursday's Child will have open doors, much less the prospect of a pool, come August."

"What? Why?"

"Money's tight, and this economy isn't helping any. Renee and I have racked our brains trying to come up with more ways—better ways—to generate funds. But, let's face it, when it comes to a choice between putting food on the table and gas in the car, and helping kids who just need a safe place to hang out, the choice of food and gas will always win. People are more cautious with their money. I don't blame them at all." She drained her glass, set it on the small white wicker table between their chairs. "Renee and I have both taken pay cuts—twice. And we run the programs as bare-bones as humanly possible. Even so..."

"And now you have Andy to consider."

"Yeah...there's that, too. I never realized how expensive it is to feed a growing boy, to clothe him when he outgrows jeans and tennis shoes nearly as fast as I can buy them."

"Terri doesn't help?"

Brianna shook her head. "No."

"Your plate is covered up."

"I'm not complaining. I love Andy, and I love what I do at the center. The kids are amazing...a real blessing."

"I know. It shows in your eyes when you talk about each one...Anna and Caleb, Lynette and Lucy, Bobby...I feel like I know them all."

"You do. You've been out there enough lately, helping. The kids love spending time with you and I appreciate it. Really, I do."

He rubbed his face and she heard the scratchiness of a five o'clock shadow. "What made you want to do it...open Thursday's Child?"

"My dad...something he said just before he died." She stared out across the front yard, through the weeping willow that veiled the milky halo of a crescent moon. "I remember it like yesterday. He told me, 'Do something that matters, Brianna. Make a difference with your life.' So, I brainstormed the best way to use my experience and my counseling degree. Renee and I were both very active working with programs that helped kids, and we knew there was a greater need than any of those programs covered. So I approached her with the idea of Thursday's Child. She's great at marketing, and she graduated top of our class in business. She was hooked from the word go. My dad left everything he had to Terri and me. It wasn't much—the house, some bank CD's—but it was enough to get things started. Terri grabbed her share, took Andy and high-tailed it to California to chase her dreams. Me, I threw everything I had into *my* dream—making Thursday's Child happen."

"And you did...make it happen."

"For now, yes. But tomorrow...?"

He reached for her hand, squeezed it gently, and the warmth of his touch, the familiar rough calluses brushing against the tender flesh of her wrist, made her shiver with longing. This was the Jackson she'd fallen in love with—the adventurous, caring boy who'd grown into a strong, gentle, and patient man. At least she'd loved him before the lure of the NFL changed him, before the promise of money and fame grabbed him with both hands and wrenched him away.

"Don't worry, Bri, it'll all work out."

"Easy for you to say." She didn't try to hide the bitterness in her voice. What did he know about financial worries? "You don't have a care in the world when it comes to money."

His eyes darkened beneath the moonlight, and shaggy waves of hair tufted beneath a slight breeze. "Maybe so. But, believe it or not, money's not everything."

"Tell that to the kids who show up to the center, come August, to the doors chained shut."

"I'm telling you, Bri, it'll be okay. Trust me."

Trust me...

She shivered, despite the humidity in the star-spattered cloak of darkness. He'd said those words once before...on a warm night much like this...and the end result was nothing less than disaster.

9

"AUNT BRIANNA, WAKE UP!" ANDY'S incessant pounding on the bedroom door startled her from a heavy slumber. His voice was muffled through the six-paneled wood. "Guess what?"

Her mind struggled to wrap itself around the challenge. She moaned and flopped onto her belly, pulling rumpled blankets over her head. "It's much too early for guessing games. Go back to bed."

The door rattled again as he pummeled it impatiently. "Jackson called."

Jackson...no.

She lifted her head long enough to glance at the clock. Eight twenty-five...what in the world? *Doesn't anybody sleep in on Saturday morning anymore?*

"Aunt Brianna, come on! Wake up." Andy threw open the door and came bounding in with Max at his side. The dog lunged onto the bed and it shook like a ten on the Richter scale, nearly toppling her to the hardwood floor. She grabbed the wrought iron headboard and hung on till the quake eased.

"Down, Max. Bad dog." She pushed sleep-tangled hair from her eyes and tried to shove him from the mattress, but it was like trying to move a brick building with a feather duster. He simply settled in the warm blankets, sighed and tucked his head against his massive front paws to stare at her with those huge golden eyes of his.

"Jackson's coming to get us in a while." Andy continued, barely taking a breath. He had already showered and dressed in his favorite jeans and the T-shirt she'd picked up for him at a clearance sale the last time they'd gone to the mall. The clean scent of soap clung to his skin and his hair was smoothed into damp caramel waves. "We're gonna hang out and eat an early lunch at Calhoun's on the river, then he's gonna take me to see the Vol's locker room and the training facilities before we head to the game. Maybe I'll even get to meet some of the players, ask for a few autographs. Isn't that cool, Aunt Brianna? I think I'll take the ball Jackson gave me, just in case." He paused for a breath, then cranked things up a notch. Leaning over the bed, he lifted the matted hair that fanned her ear and shouted, "Hey, wake up!"

She slapped a hand over each ear and cringed as a dull ache began to form at the base of her skull.

The game. Oh, no.

She'd told Jackson they weren't going, hadn't she? A groan rose from the pit of her belly. No, he'd left last night without either of them mentioning it...and they'd been talking about the center, so it's no wonder she forgot. Maybe he did, too. He seemed as caught up in the kids as she was.

Great, just great.

Andy's tennis shoes slapped the wood floor as he rounded the bed. She heard a loud *swoosh*, then a *clatter* that sounded like the house was falling down around her. A burst of stars danced before her eyes.

"Close the blinds, Andy." Her eyes burned as cheerful morning sunlight stabbed them and she rubbed furiously when her head began to pound. Beyond the window an expanse of cerulean blue sky mocked her. Not a cloud...no threat of rain in sight. Not that the threat of rain would matter any to Jackson. He'd played through some of the worst storms imaginable.

Ugh! She rolled over, buried her head beneath the pillow. Her mouth was dry, and she could use a trip to the bathroom—now. "Give me a minute here. I need to catch my breath."

"But you haven't *done* anything yet." Andy jerked the pillow from her head and pressed a mug into her hands. The rich aroma of hazelnut urged her blood to flow. "Look, I made you coffee. You like that sweetener, right? The one that comes in little pink packets? I stirred in a couple for you. Go ahead, drink."

She sat up, sipped, and blanched. The brew was way too sweet, but at least he'd tried. She took another sip, forced a swallow, and glanced over at the dog, who'd buried his nose in her side. "Well, Max, this is a fine start to the weekend." She reached to scratch his head. "At least you're sane this morning—kind of." His tail swept the rumpled blankets as he nudged her hand for more.

"You gotta get up, Aunt Brianna. Jackson's on his way."

"I heard you the first time...and the second—and the fifth." She pushed the blankets back and stretched kinks from her spine. "I don't think we should go to the game, Andy. I was planning to paint the porch today. It's in desperate need of a makeover. The neighbors are going to start leaving complaints in the mailbox."

"Jackson said you'd say that. He said you mentioned the porch last night while you two sat out front talking."

She scratched her head, smoothed tangles from sleep-matted hair. She didn't remember that part of their conversation.

"He's gonna come over one night next week to help us paint, so we don't have to do it today. He said he'd talk to you about it, work out the details, when he comes to pick us up." Andy lifted the shade on her second window, the one across from her bed. Sunlight reflected off the mirror above her dresser, magnifying in brilliance. The ache crept up the back of her head and across her temples, intensifying. She needed more coffee—not-so-sweet-it-gags-you-coffee—and fast. "Oh, he mentioned he likes pasta, so I thought when he comes to help maybe you could make that baked ziti stuff that's so good. You know—the one you sprinkle with tons of mozzarella cheese and bake in the oven?"

"Andy—"

He wrapped fingers around her arm, tugged. Coffee sloshed over the rim of the mug and splattered her pajama top. "Please, Aunt Brianna, get up."

"Oh, you win." She slung her legs over the edge of the bed and flashed him a death glare. "You just remember this the next time I wake you out of a sound sleep for school—or church—and you're all grumpy and hateful. Payback is sweet, you know, and I'm keeping tabs, buddy."

"Fine. But you'd better get moving, unless you're planning to go to the game in your pajamas. Jackson'll be here soon."

"How soon?"

She heard a car pull into the driveway, the familiar purr of the Mustang's high-dollar engine. Her hand tightened on the coffee mug.

It can't be...no way.

Andy rushed to the window. The grin that covered his face told all she needed to know. She ran a hand through her tangled hair and rubbed sleep from her eyes, mortified.

"There he is, just like he promised." He spun and raced for the doorway. "Hurry, Aunt Brianna. I'm heading outside. We're gonna pass the pigskin while you get ready."

She groaned and reached for her robe. *Pass the pigskin...the kid is hooked.*

****

Moonlight washed over the front lawn and the Mustang barely came to a stop in the driveway when Andy threw open the rear passenger door and leapt out. Sprinting to the front door, he hollered, "I gotta call Brody. He'll never believe everything we did today." He slipped his house key in the lock, pushed open the door. Before he dashed inside, he turned back, his hair like a rich wave of coffee creamer as it rustled in the breeze. "Thanks for letting me go, Aunt Brianna. This has been the most awesome day ever!"

Jackson grinned and drummed his fingers on the steering wheel. "And you thought going to the game would be a mistake."

"You were right." She sighed and eased back against the seat. "I've never seen him so excited, Jack. You've really made an impression on him."

"What about his aunt...did I impress her, too?"

"No need to impress me. You know that, Jackson. I knew you, became friends with you, when you were just the scrawny new kid on the block."

"Scrawny?" His face scrunched into a mock-scowl. "Hey, I've never been scrawny."

"Is that so?" She laughed. "In the sixth grade...hate to break it to you, but you certainly were. And I have the pictures to prove it."

"Well, then, I'm in trouble. You could leak the evidence to one of those gossip papers I see in the grocery store checkout aisles. *That* payoff would solve all of Thursday's Child's financial woes, for sure."

She sobered at the thought. "I'd never do that to you, Jack—not ever."

He eased back, stretched powerful legs beneath the dash. "I know." It was one of the many reasons he'd fallen in love with her way back when. She was loyal and honest to a fault. She'd never dream of hurting someone she loved.

Yet I hurt her. How can I reconcile that?

"Would you...like to come in for a glass of iced tea, a cup of coffee?"

"Sure, tea sounds good, if it's not too late. I know you have to get up early for church tomorrow." She'd told him she sang in the choir, and their rehearsal came before the first service. He remembered she had a pretty voice, one that used to lull him with an earthy southern cadence when she sang the most popular tunes along with his car stereo.

She glanced at the clock on the dashboard. “The carriage won’t turn back into a pumpkin for a few hours, so we’re good.”

“Okay.” He switched off the engine, tucked the keys into the front pocket of his jeans. “You *do* make some delicious iced tea.” He came around the front of the car, opened the passenger door for her.

The cool night breeze fluttered her hair as she slipped from the seat. He smelled the familiar scent of sweet vanilla on her skin. It was the same lotion she’d slathered on through high school and college...the one he liked so much...the one that made her skin silky to the touch. He shook his head, struggled to focus on what she said as he followed her up the walk and settled into a white wicker chair that flanked a small round table graced with a rainbow of potted wave petunias.

“I’ll just be a minute.” She pulled open the screen door. “Would you like some extra sugar in your tea?”

“No. The way you brew it is just right.”

The screen door slapped against its frame as she disappeared inside. He heard the clink of ice against glass, the sound of the refrigerator door swishing open and closed. Then she returned holding two tall glasses garnished with thick wedges of lemon. She offered him one before she slipped off her sandals and settled into the chair beside him with a sigh. She tucked her feet up beneath her and smoothed her denim skirt.

"Thanks." He drew a long sip. "This is great."

"You're welcome." Her voice was light, almost musical with its lilting southern accent. The sound never grew old. "Was it odd, watching the game today from the sidelines instead of running plays on the field?"

He found it difficult to gather his voice, make anything more than a croak come from his throat, as he studied the delicate hands clasped in her lap. Her fingers were bare, and he wondered what ever happened to the promise ring he'd given her. He'd spent hours agonizing over just the right setting, the perfect stone. Back then, the small amount of money he'd spent had seemed like a fortune, but he wouldn't have changed things for the world. Did she still have it, tucked safely away somewhere? Or maybe she'd flushed it down the toilet after he left that night, her face a mask of tears—good riddance.

He lightened his tone to cover the way his heart raced at the closeness of her. "It did feel a little odd, but I never knew what I was missing all those years on the field. You have quite a...um...voice." He cupped a hand to the side of his head. "I think I've lost some of the hearing in my left ear."

"Sorry. I get pretty caught up."

"I had no idea. It's hard to hear anything from the stands when you're on the field, wearing a helmet and intent on calling the perfect plays."

She gave him a wry grin. Her eyes were dark-chocolate covered almonds beneath the warm glow of moonlight. "So all that cheering I did for you over the years, all the times I suffered post-game laryngitis, was pointless?"

"Oh no, not pointless at all. I knew you were there, and it made a huge difference for me."

"How's that?"

"Just knowing you cared enough to come, to share it all with me."

"Your dad came, too. He never missed a home game. We used to sit together and share a bag of roasted peanuts."

"I know. Sometimes I'd look up through the glare of sunlight and I'd see the two of you sitting there together in a sea of orange and I'd just get...choked up. My dad always liked you. He still asks about you, from time to time."

"And you tell him...?"

"I don't know. What's there to tell? We've gone way too long without talking, Bri. I've missed it….missed you."

She stiffened in the chair, and he heard a sharp intake of breath. "I've been here. You went away."

"I know. But I'm back."

"For how long?" Disappointment flashed across her eyes. "It's been six years, Jackson. A lot has changed. *I've* changed. Things have happened...things you don't—couldn't—know anything about."

"But I want to know." He grasped her hand, held on. "You have to talk to me, Bri. You have to trust me."

"I can't...not like this." She turned her head, but not before he saw the glimmer of tears in her eyes. "It's complicated, Jackson."

He tucked his free hand beneath her chin, gently tugged her toward him. "Nothing's so complicated that it can't be worked through...worked out."

She pulled back, shook her head so silky blonde hair danced over her shoulders like a wave. A tear splashed his hand. "I used to believe that, too. But time has changed things. You leaving the way you did—that changed things, too, Jackson, at least for me. You can't just come back, show up, and think things will pick up right where they left off. It's not fair."

"I'm sorry, sweetheart."

"You've already said that. And it means a lot to me, really it does. But knowing you're sorry doesn't change what happened, and it can't change things now."

He felt like he was falling off a cliff, like the ground was coming up fast to meet him. "Maybe we could just...take things slow. See what happens."

"No!" She sprang up, paced the length of porch with a fist pressed to her mouth. "That's impossible, Jackson."

"Why, Bri?"

She turned to face him, cheeks wet with tears. Her voice was high-pitched, strained, and the melodic southern lilt was even more pronounced. "What you've done for Andy—the attention you've shown him—means the world to me. No one's been that kind to him since he moved here, or before, for that matter. And the garden at Thursday's Child...well, the kids love it. *I* love it. I'll never be able to repay you for all you've done. But nothing more can happen between us, Jackson—*nothing*." She turned toward the front door, opened the screen. It squeaked on its hinges, eerily renting the warm night air. "I'm going inside now. You...you'd better leave."

"Wait." He sprang to his feet, ignoring the sudden tug of pain in his knee. "Just give me a minute." But when he reached for her she sidestepped to the left like a startled doe.

All the times her eyes had begged him to stay...the times she'd *wanted* him...and he'd left, just like that. Now the tables were turned and he was powerless to change things.

It's like losing her all over again.

"Please, Jackson. I really have to go inside, so...goodnight."

He longed to hold her, to kiss away the doubt. In the past he might have allowed impatience to force his hand. But now, instead, he fought for strength as he swallowed hard and jammed his hands deep into his pockets.

When he spoke, his voice was gentle as the night breeze that danced around them. "Okay, sweetheart. Goodnight...for now. I'll wait while you lock up."

10

HER HEART BEAT SO FAST it threatened to leap from her chest as perspiration drowned the pink T-shirt she'd donned just thirty minutes ago, but Brianna felt like she couldn't run fast enough to chase away the demons.

"This pace is killing me, Bri." Renee's running shoes pounded the blacktopped trail as she struggled to keep up. "You've got to slow down."

Though it went against her desire to sprint until she simply dropped from sheer exhaustion, Brianna eased her speed down a few gears, into a kinder, gentler rhythm. "Sorry."

Renee fell into step beside her, arms pumping overtime, her breath coming in short, raspy gasps. "Where's the fire?"

"What fire?"

"The one you're running from."

"Oh, that." She sucked a deep breath through her nose, let it out slowly by way of her mouth as her heart rate eased with the milder pace. "Jackson took Andy and me to the Orange and White game yesterday."

"What? He what?" Renee slammed on the brakes and turned to gape, her face flushed from the warm afternoon sun. She propped her hands on her hips. "Okay, Bri, spill the beans. What's going on?"

"I don't know. You're aware Jackson's been coming by the center for a while now to play ball with the kids—"

"And to till a garden and install a sprinkler system—and he bought a truckload of new equipment for the gym."

"He did? I didn't know about that."

"Now you do."

"And he's showing Andy the ropes...teaching him football moves and stuff. They've really hit it off. Andy's like a different kid. He made A's on two projects and a math test last week."

"You're kidding, right?"

"I'm dead serious."

"That's wonderful news."

"I know. Who would have imagined that Jackson would be such a good influence on him?"

"So, what's the problem? Sounds like a good thing to me."

"On the surface, yes." Brianna shrugged, took a deep breath and motioned toward the trail. "Can we keep moving, please? I need to run."

"Okay." They eased back onto the boulevard trail. The scent of lilacs clung to a slight breeze, and cotton-candy clouds blanketed the sun. “And beneath the surface?”

Brianna struggled to let Renee set the pace, though she longed to tear things wide open. “It’ll crush Andy when Jackson leaves again.”

“Andy...or you?”

“Don’t be silly, Renee.” Brianna wasn’t sure if the strain in her voice was caused by the oppressive humidity...or the sudden onslaught of tangled emotions. “I’ve been over Jackson for a long time. It’s ancient history.”

“Is it? You can’t run away forever, Bri.”

“I’m not running away.”

“Oh, I think you are.”

Brianna’s gaze fell. She stumbled over her own two feet, caught herself before she crashed to the pavement. Her heart raced double-time as she found her footing.

“He-he told me he’s sorry...for what happened.”

Renee stopped again, grabbed Brianna’s shoulders to spin her around. “You told him...about Luke?”

She shook from Renee’s grasp and paced the pavement like a caged animal. “No. Of course not.”

“Then what is he sorry about?”

“That he hurt me. He asked me to forgive him. He wants to...spend some time together, see how things go. What am I supposed to do, Renee? After all this time, all the hurt, what do I do?"

"You're not—"

"—over him, am I?" Brianna finished with a sob. "Oh, Renee. This is...bad."

Renee uncapped her water bottle and dipped her head back to down a long swig. When she recapped the bottle and looked at Brianna again, bright green eyes held steady and true.

"I'm not downplaying what he did, Bri, or the pain you've been through. But have you ever considered—even for a moment—that he might be hurting, too?"

"No, I..."

"Thought so. Just think about it from that angle, will you?"

"I don't know if I can, Renee."

"I've been friends with you for a long time, and I knew Jackson, too, when you two were... together." She sighed and slapped her thigh. "Brianna, I think you should tell him...about what happened. About Luke."

"No!" She pressed a fist to her mouth. "I can't."

"He has a right to know. He made a child...lost a child...and he doesn't even have a clue." Renee crossed her arms, lifted her chin in a challenge. "Besides, you're still hurting, Bri, and it's not going to go away. Not until—"

She shook her head, eyes brimming with tears. "You're right. The hurt will never go away."

"But it doesn't have to hobble you, Bri."

"I'm not—" She paused, sank to a concrete bench along the running trail. Was Renee right? Was she...*hobbled*? She felt suddenly winded, like she'd just finished the last grueling leg of a marathon.

Cast your cares on the Lord and He will sustain you... Wasn't it Renee, during the darkest times, who printed Psalm 55:22 on a scrap of paper and taped it to the bathroom mirror for Brianna to see—and remember—each day?

"I have to sit for a moment, Renee. I need to sort this out. I...I need to pray."

"I'll sit here with you, Bri." Renee slipped onto the bench beside her and took her hand. "You don't have to go through this alone. I'll pray, too."

****

"What are these?" Brianna picked up one of the colorful flyers that were stacked on the lobby counter when she returned to the Thursday's Child center later that day.

"Information on a fundraiser," Renee told her. "Read it."

Brianna scanned the headline, drank in the fine-print details. She couldn't believe what she read.

"The Tennessee Vols are coming here next Saturday for a football camp and autograph signing?"

"Not all the players, just the ones who know Jackson personally."

Brianna's arms crossed defensively. She felt her gaze narrow. "Jackson—what does he have to do with this?"

"He arranged it. He's sponsoring the day, paying the expenses, and all the cash we bring in is pure profit." She took the flyer from Brianna, set it back on the stack and began to organize the information bulletins spread across the polished countertop. "The camp is already full—we have a waiting list. And I'm sure we'll have lines a mile long for autographs."

"But how? When?" Brianna sputtered. "When did you plan this, and how did it get by without me knowing?"

"Jackson approached me about it a few weeks ago. We worked through the details and he had the flyers printed up."

"Why didn't you tell me?"

"He was afraid you'd nix the idea. You haven't been very...well...cooperative with him lately."

"Cooperative—what's that supposed to mean?"

"You're angry, Bri, and it's getting in the way of everything else."

She fought the urge to stomp her foot. “I am *not* angry.”

“Okay—you’re not angry. So, go call Jackson and thank him. Oh, and tell him we can meet at two this afternoon to iron out the final details. Channel Ten News will be here at four to do an interview that will help promote the event.”

“The news—today?”

“Yeah, Bri.”

She ran a hand through her hair, still damp from the quick shower she indulged in following their run. “Renee...if you weren’t my friend I’d—”

“You can thank me later. Now, we need to go over the budget for the summer programs once more, tighten up the numbers before Jackson arrives.” She handed Brianna her cell phone. “Call Jackson—his number’s in my contact list—then meet me in my office so we can talk. Oh, and grab a couple cans of soda on your way back. That run left me parched.”

****

“The promo spot is perfect,” Jackson said as they huddled around Brianna’s desk to watch it run on the evening edition of the news. “The team really did a good job.”

“I have to agree.” Brianna sipped a diet cola. “I love the spontaneous clips they shot of the kids. It shows the heart of the reason Thursday's Child exists."

"And that footage of you tossing the ball with the kids..." Renee chimed in. "Well, it's priceless, Jackson."

He shrugged. "I can't take the credit. Andy's a natural on camera. When he's done playing football, he might have a career as an announcer." He reached for a slice of pepperoni pizza from the box that lay open across Brianna's desk. The aroma of spicy marinara sauce and garlic-glazed breadsticks filled the room. "We should have a healthy turnout if the weather cooperates."

"If not, we'll just move things indoors." Already, Brianna's mind whirled with the logistics. "We can manage that. There's plenty of space."

A shadow fell across the doorway.

"Miss Renee?" Blakely, the quiet, dark-haired college girl who worked the front counter in the evenings, rapped softly on the door. "There's someone here to see you about a summer program. He's waiting in the lobby."

"Thank you, Blakely. Tell him I'll be right there."

When she left, the room fell oddly quiet. The newscast had ended, and Brianna switched off the portable TV perched on top of a file cabinet across from her desk. She scooted into the chair across from Jackson and tried not to breathe in the scent of his aftershave or notice how the navy polo shirt intensified the mysterious smoky-gray of his eyes.

"We should have told you about the camp before...when we were planning things," Jackson said as he reached for a second slice of pizza. "Don't be mad at Renee. She wanted to say something to you, but I talked her out of it."

"It's okay." Brianna took a breadstick and bathed it in marinara sauce. "I should have told you before, when I called you earlier about our meeting, but I let my pride get in the way—thank you, Jackson. I really...appreciate what you're doing for us—for the kids."

"It's nothing, Bri. The guys—the football players—are glad to help out, and the coach gave his full support. He used to hang out at a place like this when he was young, so he understands what it's all about."

"I wish more people did. I'm afraid we're going to lose everything."

"I know. But this is a start, at least."

"A very healthy start. Thank you."

"We still make a good, team, sweetheart. Don't you think?"

Her conscience gnawed as Renee's words echoed in her head. *He has a right to know, Brianna. He made a child, lost a child, and he doesn't have a clue.*

What would it do to him if he ever *did* find out, and how could she ever bring herself to tell him?

11

THE AROMA OF SIZZLING T-BONES on the gas grill made Brianna's mouth water. She watched Jackson lean over the grill beside Andy, grab a thick steak with tongs, and demonstrate the proper flipping technique. Grilling, apparently, was a work of art for Jackson and now Andy was hooked, too.

She laughed as Max circled their feet, his jowls bubbling with slobber, hoping for a scrap of meat to fall off the bone.

He'll enjoy a nice treat later.

The oven timer buzzed, and Brianna went inside to check on the potatoes. Heat from the oven washed over her as she opened the door to prick one of the hand-selected spuds with a fork. The size of them amazed her. No cheap potatoes from one of those discount ten-pound bags she stocked up on—Jackson had hand-picked these big boys himself.

She closed the oven door, reset the timer for another ten minutes, and turned to check the table. A crisp salad filled her favorite floral-print ceramic bowl and three settings were ready for the feast.

And a fresh pitcher of Jackson's favorite sweet tea is on the counter, along with juicy lemon wedges, in case he wants to refill his glass.

She wandered into the living room and the thick odor of fresh paint greeted her as she gazed out the bay window. The porch looked new again from the double coat of creamy white latex they'd finished applying less than an hour ago.

Brianna smiled as she remembered how Jackson showed up that morning bearing a five-gallon bucket of premium outdoor paint and all the trimmings—brushes, plastic tarps, and a few pans to hold the paint.

Jackson also carried a sackful of groceries—three impossibly-thick T-bones, baked potatoes and the makings of a hearty salad.

"For a feast," he explained, handing her the sack. "When we're finished with the painting."

"Cool." Andy peeked into the bag, poked at the wrapping on one of the steaks. "I could eat one now, they look so good."

"Hold that thought. You know how to grill?"

Andy shook his head and lowered his gaze. "Never had the chance."

"No worries. We'll do it together. I'll show you the ropes. We can start by marinating the steaks so they'll be good and tender by the time we're finished painting and ready to toss on the grill."

He took Andy inside and together they'd rummaged around the kitchen like they owned the place, until they had utensils and spices strewn across the kitchen counter like a platoon of soldiers. Soon the steaks drowned beneath a sea of marinade.

Then they'd strode outside with purpose—two men bent on transforming the decaying exterior of her cozy little house.

"Can I get up on the ladder?" Andy asked. "I can slap paint on all the upper trim."

"It would make more sense for Jackson to do that, since he's taller." Brianna smoothed her T-shirt over a pair of khaki shorts, saved for work occasions like this. "You can help me with the rails, instead."

"It doesn't matter. *I* can help you with the rails, Bri." Jackson winked at Andy. "You're plenty tall enough, sport. Grab the ladder from my truck. I'll work down here, keep an eye on your aunt Brianna—quality control you know."

Andy nodded. "Yeah, right." His gaze locked with Jackson's, and Brianna imagined they'd formed some kind of friendly conspiracy. "I'll get the ladder and go around to the other side of the house, work my way toward you two, if that's okay. We can meet in the middle."

"Sounds like a good plan." Jackson pried open the paint bucket, lifted it like it weighed next to nothing. He poured a healthy amount into Andy's pan, then Brianna's and his own. "Take this."

Andy grabbed the ladder and the pan and went around to the opposite side of the house. Pressing ear buds into his ears, he cranked up the volume on his iPod and got lost in his own world.

The back door slammed, startling Brianna from the memory. "It's chow time, Aunt Brianna! Wait until you see these juicy slabs of meat."

She smelled their rich aroma and her belly unleashed a small roar. She gave the porch one last look before turning back toward the kitchen. The oven timer buzzed again...perfect. She walked through the doorway to see Jackson don oven mitts and open the door to reach into the heat.

She stopped in her tracks, let out a hearty laugh. Jackson dropped the potatoes onto the stove top and turned to look.

"What's so funny?"

"You—in those mitts."

He held them up, turned his hands this way and that for a closer inspection of the flowery cloth. "I don't see anything funny."

She laughed again, and Andy joined in.

"Don't burn your hands," Andy cautioned as Jackson tossed the foil-wrapped spuds onto a plate. "You won't be able to throw the football after dinner."

"I'm an expert." Jackson set the plate on the table. "Don't worry about my hands, sport. Just toss those steaks on the table and scrub your own, okay?"

“I’m on it.”

Brianna marveled as Andy set the platter of meat in the center of the table and rushed to the sink to lather his hands. No argument—no debate. Amazing, really.

He dried his hands and they each slid into a chair. Jackson cleared his throat and glanced at her from across the table. “Do you mind if I say grace?” He reached for her hand.

Hoping her voice didn’t give away how startled the request made her feel, Brianna answered, “Yes, please.”

“Thanks.” So the three held hands and bowed their heads as Jackson murmured a heartfelt blessing over the food.

Brianna remembered a similar time...the first time she and Jackson had prayed together.

It was the summer before their freshman year of high school, and she’d invited him to a family picnic at the lake. Baskets of hamburger buns and bowls of potato salad and baked beans graced a sunflower-yellow cloth her mom had smoothed across the picnic table. The aroma of meat made her belly dance as juicy hamburgers sizzled on the portable charcoal grill her dad saved for occasions like this.

“Brianna,” her mom called as she shooed a fly away from the platter of frosted fudge brownies. “You set the table while Jackson helps your father get the burgers from the grill. Then we’ll eat.”

Brianna hummed as she laid plastic forks and knives beside paper plates, atop paper towels she'd folded into neat little triangles. Behind her, she heard her dad teaching Jackson the ropes on grilling burgers to juicy perfection. When Jackson spoke, she noticed his voice had deepened during the past several weeks. He'd grown taller as spring eased into summer. Now, when they arm wrestled at the kitchen table during a homework break he always won.

When he brought the platter of grilled meat to the table, he grinned at her and winked. "You can have first choice, but it all looks good."

Terri and her parents joined them at the table, and Jackson surprised everyone by asking if he could say grace.

"Sure." Her mom's eyes had glowed with pride, as if he were her own son. And with as much time as Jackson spent hanging around their house he could be, except Brianna didn't think of him as a brother. She felt something different...something that made her insides sing. "You go right ahead, Jackson."

They joined hands, and she still remembered how strong and warm Jackson's fingers had felt as they twined with hers. His dark hair, damp and tousled from their swim in the lake, fell over his eyes as he bowed his head.

His words made tears well in her eyes. As she listened to him give thanks for her parents, for Terri...for her, she knew, somehow, he'd finally let go of the bitterness over the loss of his mom, a loss that had made him restless and kept him from believing in the Savior she herself had grown to love. Since the day they'd met they'd shared so many things, and now they shared a strong faith, too.

And it was his own mom's death that helped him to understand her so well when she, too, lost her mom the next spring. He was the only one who truly felt what she went through...the profound hurt and grief that plagued her during the months that followed.

Now, gazing across her own kitchen table at Jackson, she wondered what had happened to his faith when he left her for good, the night he'd boarded a plane to Jacksonville, and how, somehow, he'd seemed to find that faith once again. Would he hold onto it, grow stronger in it now, or would he pull away from it again, like he had during the NFL draft, and the years that followed?

How can I trust where this may lead, Lord? I can't bear to be hurt again.

When the prayer ended, Jackson lifted his head and his eyes found hers. He motioned to the platter that overflowed with perfectly-grilled steaks. "You can have first choice, sweetheart, but it all looks good."

****

Jackson watched Brianna plunge her arms, elbow deep, into the sudsy dish water. Finding a plate, she scoured it with a small yellow sponge, removing stubborn remnants of baked potato from the meal they'd shared.

A delicious meal, he might add.

Her posture relaxed as she leaned against the counter, and sleek blonde hair caressed the nape of her neck. There was something inherently appealing about watching a woman wash a dish, rinse it and stack it neatly in the drain...something that made his gut curl tight and his heart race.

He eased in beside her, drew a breath of the vanilla that scented her skin, and reached for a dish towel.

"Mind if I help?"

"I'd...like that."

The kitchen's cabinet space was limited, so it wasn't hard to put things back in their proper place. "Andy's football skills have improved by leaps and bounds." He glanced through the window over the sink. "And he's tumbled head-first into a growth spurt, which is a huge plus. Look at him handle the ball."

"He *has* gotten better," Brianna followed his gaze. "You've really helped him, Jackson."

"I can't take the credit. He's practiced a lot."

"True. But you believe in him, and that gives him the confidence to keep trying, to work harder."

She handed him another plate. “Mr. Grinstead called this afternoon.”

“Oh, no. What now?”

She grinned. “Relax. It was nothing like that. He just wanted to tell me how much Andy’s improved. He’s turning in all of his work on time this grading period and he’s making an A, Jackson. Isn’t that wonderful?”

“Yes, that’s certainly good news.”

“The best.”

“So, I guess this means he gets to help with the camp tomorrow? He’s been looking forward to working with the guys from UT.”

“I know, and yes, he’ll be there to help. We’ll both be there bright and early.”

“Then, I guess I’d better head on home and let you get some sleep. It’s getting late.”

“It is, Jackson.” She rinsed the last dish, and he dried it before placing it into a cabinet. “Thank you for painting...for dinner...for everything.”

“You’re...welcome.” He tucked a strand of hair behind her ear, and her eyes widened to the size of chocolate kisses as his knuckles brushed her cheek. “You’re beautiful, Bri.”

“I...” She stepped back and pressed a hand to the side of her face. The pink tinge of blush swept across her cheeks. “I’ll walk you to the door.”

Before the screen door slapped closed behind him, he turned to face her. He cleared his throat, shifted feet as he gathered the words he needed to say. "You know that night—when we..."

Her gaze lowered and the pink tinge exploded to full-blown crimson. "Yes, Jackson, I remember."

"I-I'm sorry it happened the way it did. I know you wanted...to wait. I pushed you, Bri, and I shouldn't have. It...I was wrong."

"It's done, Jackson. We can't go back."

"I know. I just wanted to...tell you that. You should know that, Bri."

His gut clenched as her eyes filled with tears. There was more she longed to say...he could sense it.

"You should go now, Jackson."

He didn't want to—could hardly bear the thought. But she was right...he should go.

"Goodnight, sweetheart." *I love you.* The words almost slipped out, but he held his tongue. "Sleep well, and I'll see you in the morning."

"Yes, Jackson...in the morning."

****

Brianna stared up at the ceiling through the stillness of her bedroom. Moonlight peeked through the blinds, casting an eerie glow. She thought of Jackson, and sleep refused to come. Memories of that night, the one Jackson had referred to, came tumbling back to her.

There'd been a storm...one that caused the earth to shake with deafening roars of thunder and the skies to flash with heated streaks of lightening. And the wind...it had swirled and moaned restlessly around the small campus house Jackson rented with two other players.

There was a break in training and his roommates were gone for the weekend—home to visit their families. She and Jackson were alone, and the storm held them prisoner. When the power went out, Jackson rummaged through the kitchen drawers until he found some votive candles. Soon, light warmed the room and their shadows flickered along the walls.

"I should go," she said after a while. "It's getting late. Renee will be worried."

"You can't go out in this." Concern filled his eyes as he drew her close. His body, strong from hours spent in the gym and thousands of plays on the field, was like hot steel against her. "It's dangerous."

"It's dangerous here, too." The candlelight lulled her, and she felt her resistance fading. She murmured breathlessly into his soft cotton T-shirt. "Take me home, Jackson. Please."

Instead he kissed her while thunder crashed around them and lightening rent the room. Soon, the rain rushed down in torrents, filling the gutters so water gushed into the front yard like a river. Inside her, desire flooded over as well.

Jackson's mouth demanded, his hands explored in ways that ignited a longing she was powerless to resist...and then suddenly it was too late.

Afterward they were both deathly quiet...knowing they'd broken a promise to themselves, to each other—to God, and that there was no going backwards, no undoing what they'd done.

"I love you, Brianna," Jackson had finally whispered across the darkness—the candles had long since flickered cold, like the chill that seemed to bury itself deep in her bones. His words did little to ease the ache in her heart. "This doesn't change anything."

Oh, but it did. It changed everything.

12

JACKSON SLID INTO BRIANNA'S OFFICE chair and propped his feet on her desk in a way she'd become accustomed to over the past month. She had to admit, he looked good relaxing there. He tucked his hands behind his head, showing off the muscular arms he'd spent hours and hours honing to the perfect strength. "So, what's the bottom line?"

The eerie hum of air-conditioning fans forced cool air through the office wing. Renee had left ten minutes ago, after sharing a quick and quite promising financial update. Though exhausted from the long day of hard work, Brianna felt a weary smile spread across her face. "The day was a huge success. I've never seen so many people line up for autographs! Most of them slipped donations into the jar Renee thought to place on the table, as well."

Jackson adjusted his huge frame in her small chair, and the springs squealed under the stress of his weight. "Yes, it was a generous crowd, for sure."

"The players were so gracious and patient with the kids. They must have signed a thousand photos."

"Not to mention the footballs, hats and T-shirts kids carried along, too."

"Right." Brianna ran a hand over one of the neon-green T-shirts Jackson had printed up with the Thursday's Child logo. The color would certainly stand out in a crowd, adding to the exposure the program so desperately needed. He'd donated three-dozen boxes of them to hand out at the signing—over a thousand shirts. "We won't have a complete profit report until Monday, but Renee said she thinks we've made enough to fund all the summer programs. Now, we just have to work on the building lease."

"The lease?" Jackson shifted in the chair and crossed his ankles on the cluttered desk, nudging aside a paperweight. "What's going on with that?"

Brianna slipped into the armchair across from him and stretched the kinks from her aching back. "The owners have decided to sell this property when the two-year lease we signed expires in August. We have the first right of purchase, but our funds are seriously lacking. Without a miracle, we're going to lose the building completely."

"No." The chair protested as Jackson sat up suddenly, his eyes dark and serious. "That can't happen."

It was obvious he'd become as attached to and protective of the kids as she was. "I hope it doesn't, but yes, it *can* happen."

"Then what?" His eyes searched hers.

She shrugged as a lump formed in her throat. She didn't like to think about the what-if's, but she knew all too well they were very real possibilities. "We close the doors, unless we can find another location. And believe me, Jackson, Renee and I have spent hours scouring the surrounding area. There's nowhere else that's both suitable *and* within our price range. If there was, we'd have found it by now. We need to come up with a way to buy this building outright, to stay here. It's a great location...perfect for our needs and the kids' needs, as well."

"There has to be a way." Jackson rubbed a hand across his chin, shadowed with stubble.

"If there is, I have yet to find it." The thought of closing the doors to Thursday's Child sickened Brianna, and she didn't want to spoil such a perfect day with worry and doubts. So she changed the subject before sadness overwhelmed her and ferreted away the joy. "The Channel Ten News Team sure came through again for us. They recorded some great footage of you and some of the other players with the kids. I think they're going to air a segment each night this week."

"Good idea." Jackson reached for a miniature chocolate bar from the candy dish on her desk. He unwrapped it and tossed it into his mouth. His voice was jumbled around the sweet confection, and Brianna remembered how much he liked dark chocolate...and cherry-flavored gum. "That will keep public awareness heightened."

"I know. They're going to keep our website posted, too. Hopefully, some more donations will come in."

"I'm sure they will."

Jackson turned his attention to her office window. Outside the sky darkened with the first hint of nightfall. Swirls of pink and gold danced together along the horizon like ribbons in a breeze. "Where's Andy?"

"He's spending the night at Brody's house. Those two have become fast friends. I'm glad. Andy's had a hard time making friends since he came here."

"Brody seems like a nice kid. He and Andy sure had a good time helping the players run the clinic."

"They did a great job, too. Andy's a natural with the little kids."

"I know." Jackson reached for a second piece of chocolate. "Who would have guessed?"

"I'll bet he and Brody won't get a wink of sleep all night, judging by how hyped up they were when they left here."

Jackson laughed and stuffed the candy into his mouth, then crumpled the wrapper and banked a shot off her desk into the trash can. “Maybe so, but a little lost sleep won’t hurt them. It’s almost summer vacation, right?”

“Right...just a few more days of school. Thank goodness. I’m as tired of homework as Andy is.”

“Summertime gets even busier here, doesn’t it?”

“You’d better believe it. We have extended hours and about four times the number of programs we offer while school’s in session.”

His gaze met hers, held. Brianna saw a question there, and held her breath, waited. “Then let me take you to dinner before the work onslaught begins. We might not have another chance for a while, and I don’t know about you, but after the long day we’ve had, I’m starving.”

She hesitated, shook her head slightly as she drew in air once again. “I...Thank you for offering, Jackson, but I’d better not.”

He pushed back from the desk and stood up.

His eyes were tender, not accusing as he came toward her. His voice was full of the gentleness she remembered...and missed so much. “Why not? What are you holding back, Bri? What are you hiding?”

“Hiding? I’m not—” She stopped mid-phrase. To finish the sentence would result in a lie, and she refused to do that. He deserved better and she would give it to him...when the time was right. *If* it was ever right. She turned from him to pace the tile floor. "I don't want to talk about it, Jackson. Not now."

"No?' He reached out to touch her arm and slowly she turned back to him. "Then, when?"

"I don't know. Just not...now." She shrugged off his touch and crossed her arms tight. "It's been a long day. We're both tired. We should both just go home, Jackson. The day's been wonderful and I don't want to...ruin it."

"Ruin it?" His gray eyes darkened with hurt. "How would going to dinner with me ruin it?"

"You know how, Jackson." It was so plain to her, how could he not see it?

"No, I don't." He sighed and ran a hand through shaggy waves of hair. "It's killing me inside, Bri. I can't stand to watch you hurt, to feel you struggling so hard to keep your distance from me, and not know why. I mean...I know I hurt you, leaving the way I did, but we've been here now, together, for a good while now and I feel...well, I know you feel it, too. So there's more. There has to be more."

Her eyes filled with tears. "Jackson, please..." Instinctively, one hand splayed over her belly and she remembered the slight bulge that had once formed there—proof of the precious life that had grown inside her.

Jackson's gaze slid over the hand she'd pressed to her midsection and his eyes narrowed with concern. "Are you okay?"

She lowered her gaze and quickly removed the hand. "I...no, I'm not okay, Jackson."

He reached for her once more, and she could smell sweet chocolate on his breath, the musky scent of a hard day's work that clung to his T-shirt. "What is it? What's wrong?"

She shook her head. Tears spilled over as he drew her close. She pressed her cheek against his chest and shuddered. Slowly the words came...words she'd held prisoner for so long, words she thought she'd never share with him. "Jackson, I-I was pregnant."

He stiffened, and she felt his heartbeat quicken beneath the thin fabric of his T-shirt. She pulled back and saw his eyes were wide with shock. "*Was* pregnant? What are you talking about?"

"Six...years ago. I got pregnant."

Rage darkened his eyes. He grasped her arms and spat, "Who's the guy, Brianna? I'll hurt him."

Her breath caught. She took a single step back. "You, Jackson." Her voice was eerily quiet. "The guy was you."

He could not have looked anymore shocked if lightening itself had struck him dead-on. He sputtered, "What? How?"

She leveled him a look. "That night...in the storm...have you forgotten?"

"The storm?" He turned, stumbled a few steps, and steadied himself with one hand on the wall. "No, of course not. But we couldn't—we only—"

"It only takes once."

"Oh, sweetheart." He dropped his head into his hands and moaned. "What happened? Where is...?"

"He? Luke. His name was Luke, Jackson. And he was still-born. I lost him four and a half months into the pregnancy."

Silence rushed in to fill the room, and Brianna thought she might suffocate. She watched a flash of emotions play across Jackson's face as he stopped breathing for a moment, his body stiff, hands clenched into tight fists.

"I don't understand. Why didn't you tell me?"

"I wanted to. I tried, but you..."

His gaze held hers, black with a million questions. His voice came quick, rough now, accusing with the temper that threatened to bite her. She knew his temper well, saw it displayed on the practice field and during games that weren't going well. But not with her...never with her. Until now. "Finish the sentence, Brianna. I what?"

"You...you didn't love me, Jackson. Not the way I...needed. All you talked about was the draft, all the money you were going to make, the fame. You never asked me—"

"Asked you what?"

"To go to Jacksonville with you. So I knew...I wasn't what you wanted."

"I loved you, Brianna. I wanted you to come with me. But I thought you wanted to stay here. You told me that often enough."

Had she? Everything seemed fuzzy now, blurred with the passage of time.

"You didn't want me with you." She shook her head, refusing to believe him. Words came easily, but the actions...not so much. "Especially not with a baby."

"How do you know?" His voice rose, and the room seemed to shrink and darken. Suddenly Brianna's chest tightened and the breath went out of her. "How dare you make that decision for me. You had no right."

She fought for air and finally drew in a quivering breath. "I-I know that now, Jack. But I didn't think—"

He looked stunned. "No, you *didn't* think." He paced the floor as the revelation began to sink in. When he spoke again she wasn't sure if he was talking to her or himself. "I had a son, and I didn't even know. How can that possibly be?"

She reached for him. "Please, Jackson—"

But it was his turn to pull away. "I thought you knew me, Bri. All the days we spent together, all the times we shared. When I told you I loved you, did you think I was just feeding you a line?"

"No...yes...oh, I don't know."

"You don't know?" He turned, slammed a fist against the wall. When he spun back his eyes were filled with tears. The sight startled her. She hadn't seen him cry since...well, since the night he'd told her the horrible way his mom had died. "And all the times you told me...that you loved me—was that just a line, Brianna?"

"No! I did...*do* love you, Jackson."

I love him. The realization took her breath away. The room began to swim. She grabbed the edge of the desk and held on.

"Don't say it. Not now. You couldn't love me and keep something like this from me. It's...impossible."

"I did what I thought was best for us, Jackson—for you."

"Don't lay that guilt trip on me, Brianna. I don't deserve it."

"Okay, then...if I'd told you...about Luke, would you have stayed? Would you have given up your dream for a baby? For me?"

"I...I—" He paced the floor, his long stride eating up the tile. "I guess we'll never know, will we?" Suddenly he swung away from her and started toward the door.

She wanted to follow him, but the room went dark and hot around her. Her breath came in short, raspy gasps as beads of perspiration ran down her back. "Where are you going?"

He ran a hand through his hair, then clenched both fists so she thought he might pummel the wall again. He paused briefly at the doorway, his back to her. "I need some air. I need time to think, to sort this all out."

She stumbled toward him, caught the edge of the desk again when she felt the floor collapse beneath her feet. "I'm sorry, Jackson."

Bitterness filled his voice and echoed through Brianna's head as if from far, far away. "It's too late for sorry, Bri."

"But you said—"

"Forget what I said." He started walking again, and she heard his footsteps fade down the hall along with his voice. "I was wrong—dead wrong."

****

Jackson's world shattered. Everything he'd believed in, everything he'd trusted, was as good as gone.

Brianna had a baby...my baby...and I didn't even know.

The thought roared through his head like a wave rushing in and out. He crossed the vacant parking lot beneath a moonlit sky and fell to his knees beside the Mustang as a bout of sickness overwhelmed him.

Brianna had a baby.

When the nausea finally passed, he wiped his mouth with the back of his hand and dug in his jeans pocket for the ignition key. Despite the cool night air, he felt hot and feverish. He jammed the key into the car's lock, swung open the door and settled into the driver's seat to crank the air to full blast. Ah...relief.

Brianna miscarried a baby...my baby...Luke.

The air cooled him, chased away optic stars that danced before his eyes. He gunned the engine and the Mustang's tires squealed in protest as he raced from the lot. The acrid odor of burning rubber filled the air, mirroring the bitterness that burned a hole through his gut.

He drove through deepening darkness, not sure where he was headed. His mind was filled, yet vacant at the same time. How was that possible?

The cell phone he'd left in the console vibrated, rattling the plastic like gunshots. He grabbed it, flipped it open.

"Brianna—"

Stan's voice shouted over the line. "Jackson, what's going on there?"

The breath went out of him like a helium balloon deflating. Disappointment wrestled with bitterness. “I can’t talk right now.”

“Too busy running plays with some snot-nosed kids? I just saw the highlights on ESPN. What’s going on there? You’re making the team look bad, Jackson. You’re supposed to be on a strict training regimen and healing that knee.”

ESPN? He cringed. *News really does travel fast. Good for Brianna and Thursday’s Child...not so good for me.*

“They’re not snot-nosed kids and I *have* been training.” His voice was clipped. The last thing he needed right now was to deal with Stan’s annoying questions. “The knee *is* healing Stan.”

“Looked that way from what I saw on the news. So the owner wants to know—why aren’t you here, practicing with the team?”

“Are you insinuating...does he think—?”

“We need you back here quick, Jackson. Coach wants to talk to you. Come right away—*now*.”

“I can’t.” He’d drive around until he cooled off, then figure out what to do next, examine his options. Already he regretted the harsh words he’d slung at Brianna—again. He had to make things right.

But how can I make them right? She had a baby...my baby...and she didn’t even tell me.

“This isn’t a multiple choice question, Jackson. It’s serious. You need to come now.”

"Nothing can be that serious, Stan."

"Oh, believe me, this is."

Jackson slammed on the brakes, swerved to change direction. They wanted him now, they'd get him now. "Okay, I'm on my way. But let's make it quick, Stan. I've got things to take care of here."

"What could be more important than football?"

What could be? The question bit at him. He remembered Brianna asking..."*When will you go back?*"

He disconnected without responding and sped through the dark of night toward the airport, even though a voice inside him screamed to slow the car, park long enough to think things through. He'd left once before in a rush. It was foolish to make the same mistake twice.

Jackson ignored the voice and gunned the engine. No sense stopping by his apartment to pack a bag when he'd find everything he needed at the house in Jacksonville.

Well, almost everything.

13

"HAVE YOU HEARD FROM HIM yet?" Renee asked as she poured another cup of Orange Pekoe tea. The crisp, citrusy scent filled the room.

"No." Brianna tossed a spoonful of sweetener into her cup and stirred absentmindedly. Outside the kitchen window huge droplets of rain splattered the deck and rushed down the gutters Jackson had cleaned just a few weeks ago, before they'd given the porch a facelift together. Wind made the trees dance in an odd rhythm and the murkiness of the cloud-filled sky mirrored the darkness in her heart. "Not a thing."

"Maybe he just needs some time to sort things out." Renee offered her an oatmeal-raisin cookie she'd warmed in the microwave, but despite the rich cinnamon scent Brianna simply shook her head. Even the thought of food made her stomach revolt. "You know, Bri, you've had years to sift through what happened—losing Jackson and then Luke, too. And you did sort of dump everything in Jackson's lap last night."

"I know...you're right." She set the teaspoon down and stared at the steaming liquid in her mug. "I didn't mean for it to happen that way. It just..."

"I know. How's Andy taking it...Jackson leaving?"

"He's crushed. They were supposed to run some plays today after church. He's grown to trust Jackson, but now..." Brianna felt tears fill her eyes and threaten to spill like the fat raindrops that raced down the kitchen window. "Jackson's just another adult who's left him without so much as a goodbye. And it's all my fault, Renee. I've made such a mess of things."

Renee picked up the mug full of steaming tea and pressed it into Brianna's hands. "Drink. It's going to be okay. You'll see."

He asked me to forgive him and I refused to answer. Now, can he forgive me?

Brianna wrapped her fingers around the smooth ceramic. The warmth did little to soothe her bruised heart. "I don't think so. Not this time." She sighed. "I've lost Jackson for good now. And after all this time, how can it still hurt so much?"

"Because you love him, Bri." Renee laid a hand on her shoulder, squeezed gently. "I don't think you ever stopped loving him."

****

The tension in the room was palpable. Jackson rubbed his tired eyes and felt his knee throb beneath the khaki pants that covered his healing scar. The pain made him remember the good time he'd had with Brianna yesterday, running the clinic...signing autographs...watching kids' faces light up with the flash of a smile as he handed them one of the T-shirts he'd printed. And he remembered the way the night had ended...with harsh words and tears, and a turbulent flight through storm-filled skies.

"Did you hear me, Jackson?" Coach Donaldson—a guy he'd run plays for, given his heart and soul to—rapped his knuckles on the desk to get his attention.

Yes, I heard.

He drew a long breath, gave his temper a moment to ease down from the flash-point before he responded. When he did, the even tone of his voice masked anger boiling just beneath the surface. He clasped his hands in his lap to keep from wrapping them around someone's throat. "What do you mean, you're releasing me from my contract?"

"What part don't you understand?" Coach tucked his hands behind his head and leaned back in his chair so his ample gut rose up like a mountain. He spoke as if they were having a pleasant discussion about the weather instead of an ugly ambush concerning Jackson's NFL future. His tone rang matter-of-fact, which merely steeped Jackson's growing irritation.

Jackson dug in his pocket for a stick of gum, unwrapped it and shoved it between his teeth. The cherry flavor filled his mouth and he worked the sticky mass into submission as his hands clenched into tight fists in his lap. "Explain it once more."

"It's simple, Jack. The Seahawks need a quarterback, and they've expressed interest in a trade."

"Good for them." Suddenly restless as a caged lion, he leaned forward, propped his elbows on the desk. "But, what if I don't want to go?"

The panel of bigwigs—owner, Coach, and Stan, his agent—exchanged worried glances, then turned to gape at him as if he'd lost his mind. Coach eased further back into his chair with a nonchalance that said he'd rather be napping. He scratched his chin, cleared his throat. His gaze fell away. "It's a done deal. They're expecting you to report tomorrow."

"Tomorrow...?"

"Yes, Jack. It's all in the contract. Give it a read and you'll see." He slapped the desk, signaling a sudden end to the discussion. "I think we've chewed over this enough. It's time to move on. Look on the bright side. Seattle's a nice town...if you can overlook the rain. And playing there will guarantee you won't have to ride the bench. *And* the pay's not bad, either.

With endorsements, you should be able to continue the lifestyle you've become accustomed to." He twined his fingers over the mound of his belly and leveled Jackson a challenging look. "You could have done a lot worse."

A lot worse? They were selling him out...trading him to Washington...clear across the country from Knoxville. He was no longer a Jaguar, no longer part of the team he loved, starting tomorrow...

Jackson felt the room swim. His vision went dark for a moment before he reigned in his rage at being tossed aside like yesterday's newspaper. The years he'd given...years of hard work and sweat. Not to mention the all the sacrifices. It had meant more to him than just the money. And this was all he had to show for it? He looked at Stan, his insides churning like someone had stoked a bonfire in his belly. "I need some time to think."

"You don't *have* time, Jackson." Stan tapped a pen on the desktop and pointed to the contract that had been drawn up—a thick stack of pages bound tightly together. It would take hours to read through all the mind-numbing legalese.

"I'm not signing that until I give it a thorough read—and maybe not even then."

"You don't have to read it—I already have, and it's good. Fair."

"Fair? How can any of this be fair?"

"Trust me, Jackson. I said I've read through it." Stan's eyes narrowed. "We need to sign—now. There's no more time."

He's already read it? Then he must have known for a while this was coming down the pike. Trust him?

Chair legs scraped the marred tile floor as Jackson stood to face them all. He tossed his wadded gum wrapper on the desk and grabbed the contract. "Make time, Stan, because I'm not signing anything right now—maybe not at all."

****

Brianna heard the front door open and waited for the *slam* followed by the rattling of the front windows she'd become accustomed to when Andy kicked it closed with his foot. But no slam came, no rattling, nothing but the sharp click of the metal latch.

"Hey." He wandered onto the back deck and slipped into the chair beside her. Max moved over to prop his head on a knee in anticipation of a good ear-scratching. Andy didn't disappoint, and the mutt's tail thumped the deck wildly. "The rain's cleared up—finally. It's been raging for two whole days now. I thought it would never stop."

"Me, too." His observation reminded her it had been two days since Jackson left—two long days. How many times had she picked up her cell phone, tapped in his number, and then changed her mind just as she hit the send button?

"We're gonna have to mow again soon. Rain's made the grass look like a miniature jungle. Another day or two and Max might get lost in it."

"Don't worry about it now." She remembered how Jackson had surprised her the day he'd shown up to mow, and the way they'd shared a meal of tacos and some good conversation, just like they had...before.

She willed her mind to go blank as she sipped iced tea. The scent of lilies blooming along the fence sweetened the air and oppressive humidity lifted to make way for a cool breeze. Andy stretched his legs beside her, and she noticed the growing gap between the hem of his jeans and his scuffed tennis shoes. He was in the throes of a growth spurt, and he'd need new clothes soon. Dollar signs danced before her weary eyes. "How was your last day of school?"

"Okay...fine." He handed her his grade card. "Guess you'll be asking for this. Might as well hand it over now."

Her heart sank. The last week had been so busy planning Thursday's Child's summer programs and helping with the football camp and signing that she hadn't had as much time to help him complete his schoolwork and study for final tests. Now guilt from the neglect nudged her. "Oh, Andy, is it...?"

"Bad?" His eyes twinkled with mischief. He shrugged. "I dunno. See for yourself."

She pulled the card from its folder to study it. "Wow, Andy, it's..."

"Pretty good, huh?" He sat just a little bit taller in the chair. "I can do most of my homework by myself now, Aunt Brianna. You don't need to babysit me at the kitchen table anymore."

"You made the honor roll."

"I know. Mr. Grinstead said my name's gonna be in the newspaper when they print the semester honor roll and it won't say 'most wanted' underneath, either." He laughed at the corny joke.

She laughed, too, and the emptiness that had plagued her the past few days lifted a bit. She threw her arms around him and hugged hard. He didn't pull back...that was progress. "Oh, I'm so proud of you."

"Yeah." He sighed and pressed the toe of his tennis shoe into the crack between two drying slats of wood. "I wish Jackson was here to see it, too. Has he called yet?"

"No." Brianna sucked in a breath, let it out slowly, as the emptiness took hold once again. "I know you'd like him to see your grade card. I'm sorry he's not here."

"It's not your fault."

Oh, but it is.

"He promised to help me with my football moves." Andy's voice cracked with disappointment. "Now I'll never make the team."

Brianna patted his knee. "You will, Andy. You can do it. You might have to work a little harder and figure more out on your own, but you can do it. I believe in you."

"Well...you're the only one."

"No. Jackson believes in you, too."

He shrugged. "Yeah, right. But he's not here, so what does it matter?"

"It still matters, Andy. And you'll win the coach over, too, when he sees how hard you work. You'll see."

He ran a hand through his hair. "Do you think I can go for a haircut again? Summer practice starts tomorrow, and it's getting kind of shaggy."

"So you want to get scalped again?" Brianna smiled. "Sure. We can go right now, and then I'll take you to dinner. Tomorrow's a big day at the center. We might not have time to squeeze in a haircut."

"Can we go to Bellacino's? I love that place. The garlic knots slathered in marinara sauce are so good."

Brianna recalled the lovely dinner Jackson had ordered in for them on an evening not so long ago, and had to force back a sob.

"You bet." She sniffled softly as she swiped at her eyes. "Let me just grab my purse."

As she stood, Max did a slow circle about her feet, sniffing for crumbs from the turkey sandwich she'd nibbled earlier. She stepped over him and carried Andy's grade card into the kitchen.

Andy followed her. His tennis shoes slapped the tile floor she'd spent half an hour scrubbing that afternoon. The mindless work had eased her jangled nerves.

"What are you doing?" He watched her peel a magnet from the refrigerator door.

"Putting this in a place of honor." She grinned through a sudden wave of sadness as she hung the card beside the photo Jackson had snapped of them while their faces were smudged with white paint from their work on the porch.

He smiled. "That looks good. Thanks."

"We'll get a few copies of the newspaper, too, when it comes out. We can mail one to your mom."

"What about Jackson?"

Brianna's voice caught. "I-I guess we can mail a copy to him, too."

****

Jackson tossed the contract onto the coffee table and stood to pace the room. His footsteps echoed off the walls, reminding him just how alone he was in this sprawling house. He fumbled for the remote and switched on the TV that boasted surround-sound, just to have some background noise for company.

He wondered what Brianna was doing. A quick glance at his watch told him the summer programs at the center were in full swing. He dug in his pocket for his cell phone, punched in her number, but paused just before hitting the send button.

What should I say?

The question had plagued him for days now.

Once the shock and anger faded, disappointment and remorse took up residence in the empty crevices of his wounded heart. Brianna didn't trust him...hadn't believed he'd loved her enough to share her most intimate secret.

So she'd borne the pain and devastation of losing a child—their child...Luke—alone. What must it have been like, to feel life growing inside her one day and then nothing but emptiness the next?

He guessed he knew a little of the feeling, because his heart broke now for the loss...for all the what-if's and might-have-been's. He replayed her words over and over in his mind. What would he have done if he *had* known about Luke? How would he have handled things?

I'll never know now.

What kind of man was he, to make Brianna feel the way she did, to keep her from trusting him after all the time they spent together, after all they'd shared? The realization of his short-comings was like a stab to his very core.

He stared through the wall of glass that ran the length of his living room, to the shimmering water of an expansive kidney-shaped pool beyond. How many parties had he hosted along that pool deck? How many nights had he watched his teammates, his friends, party through the night, straight into dawn and still he felt alone, despite the crowd, because Brianna was missing...tucked safely back in Knoxville and going about her life without him? He'd lost count a long time ago.

Oh, the tabloids would have people think he led a life filled with women and excitement around every bend in the road. And he had...at the beginning. It was a heady feeling to walk out of the locker room following a game, win or lose—it didn't matter—and have pretty women falling over themselves for a chance to get close to him.

And he'd let a few, in the beginning. But each time left him feeling emptier than the time before, and the excitement faded just as quickly as it had come. Now the memories only sickened him. None of the women, no matter how appealing on the outside, held a candle to Brianna. She knew him like no one else ever had—before or since. She was beautiful from the inside out, and she'd loved him before he became...all of this.

He remembered the first time he told her he loved her. He'd had his driver's license for a year, and had saved enough money bagging groceries at the local Kroger to buy a battered pick-up truck that he and his dad spent hours restoring.

Brianna was the first one he took for a drive in it. They went down to the river and parked beneath the shade of a giant oak. While the patter of a summer rainstorm drummed over the roof and splashed the windshield, they listened to the soft hum of music from the stereo his dad had helped him install just that morning.

She was dressed in a soft cotton sundress with peach-colored flowers that brought out the rich brown of her eyes, and coral-painted toes peeked between the straps of pretty sandals on her feet.

The light fragrance of vanilla lotion on her skin mingled with the scent of his cherry-flavored gum, and humidity from the afternoon rain steamed the windows and warmed the cabin of the truck.

"I like the rain," she'd murmured.

"Yes." It was the only syllable he could force from his throat. His heart raced so fast he wondered if she could feel it shaking him—shaking the truck.

He took her hand and held it, so soft and delicate in his. When she tipped her head and her gaze met his, he saw the longing there, a mirror of his own desire. He leaned in, and her breath was warm on his cheek. Her free hand searched and twined along the hair at the nape of his neck while his lips found hers. The scent of her made him dizzy with longing, and he nearly lost himself to the need.

She sighed beneath his touch, and he knew they'd tumbled into something new, something equally wonderful and dangerous. A fierce need to protect, to treasure, rose up to mingle with the longing. After all the time they'd spent together, all they'd shared, the words came as easy as breathing. "I love you, Brianna."

She'd trembled against him and her breath caressed his ear. "Oh, Jackson, I love you, too."

Jackson remembered how her chocolate eyes grew round and huge with trust. Yet, in the end, he'd betrayed her. Oh, the kiss had long-since passed when he moved to Jacksonville, and they were no longer dating, no longer engaged. They barely spoke and even that fizzled with time. Even so, his actions over the years felt like a betrayal—to him, at least.

The massive house he bought, with the architecturally-designed pool and a media room boasting theater seating and a flat screen TV that covered an entire wall brought a small thrill, but even that faded as quickly as a suntan in the dead of winter. He found the house echoed eerily as he puttered through it, and no amount of furnishings and high-tech gadgets seemed to fill the emptiness.

He began calling his dad more often, and their evenings became filled with long conversations about nothing...and everything. From time to time Dad asked if he'd spoken to Brianna lately, and he became an expert at dodging the question, changing the subject.

He couldn't talk to her. What was there to say?

One night while he was packing for a road trip he found the Bible he'd stuffed into the dresser beneath a tangled pile of athletic socks and T-shirts. He dusted it off and settled in the quiet of his media room, alone, when none of the movies in his massive collection appealed to him.

And when he opened the Bible, the verse he turned to was like a punch to his gut, the wake-up call he needed. He read the words twice, three times.

The boundary lines have fallen for me in pleasant places; surely I have a delightful inheritance. Psalm 16:6

The words shamed him. Where were his boundary lines? What had happened to the strong convictions—the honor—he'd lived by all the years he and Brianna had shared such a sweet friendship...then a deep love?

He'd allowed the desire for money and fame to consume him, and the boundary lines had eroded. Oh, he'd made a million excuses over the years...he'd worked hard to get this far, to earn the money that was thrown at him like confetti at a parade...he *deserved* a little recognition...Brianna was living her life without him, and he owed it to himself to go on...what was one more drink, one more woman, one more late night on the town? He still gave the crowd their money's worth on Sunday afternoon, didn't he?

They'd been a long string of lies to soothe the ache in his heart that would not seem to ease. It left no room for the truth—truth that he'd become a man who dishonored the faith and beliefs by which he'd once lived so strongly.

He'd spent the night reading passages, held the Bible close to his heart like an old friend. In the morning, the dawn awakened with an explosion of color more brilliant than he'd ever seen.

When he took the field for practice that day, the game held new meaning. Over the course of the next few seasons, he became a leader who was admired and respected—not for his elaborate parties and expensive possessions, but for his dedication to his teammates and to the sport.

His game improved, and endorsement offers flowed like water from a fall. He was comfortable in front of the camera, and he thought maybe it was time to put some of his money to good use. He began researching charities, pitched a few ideas to his dad, who helped him sort through all the possibilities.

Then he got blindsided during the playoffs. Long nights filled with nagging pain followed a complicated surgery, and his only relief came from colorful pills in a little amber bottle. The temptation was too great to deny, and when the boundaries began to blur once again, he knew where he needed to go.

Home. To Knoxville...to Brianna.

But coming home had only shown him just how far he had yet to go to become the man God meant for him to be. When Brianna needed him, he responded with temper and impatience. When she shared her deepest hurt, he fired accusing words, turned and fled...just like he'd done before.

I left her alone to grieve...again.

14

"BRIANNA, WE'RE BURSTING AT THE seams with kids." Renee took a healthy bite of her roast beef sandwich, and juice from a ripe tomato dribbled down her chin. She dabbed with a wadded napkin, then chewed and swallowed before continuing. "It's amazing, truly. We're going to have to hire an additional counselor, maybe even two."

"How will we manage that?" Brianna's stomach twisted into an uneasy knot. She stood to pace the office floor. "We already hired one extra counselor and we don't have the money for another. Our budget is tapped, as it is. You know that better than anyone, Renee."

She shrugged, stuffed another bite of sandwich into her mouth. "We'll just have to find a way. You know, we promised ourselves when we started things here that the safety of the kids would always come first."

"You're right." Brianna splayed a hand across her belly to ease the rumbling. "Grab a pad of paper and a pencil. Let's brainstorm again."

"Not before you eat something." Renee pressed half of her sandwich into Brianna's hands. "You can't go on like this—skipping meals. It's wearing you down."

"I'm not hungry. I'm..."

"Look, it's been nearly a week. Maybe you should call Jackson, just to check on him."

"I can't. If he wants to talk, he'll call me. He needs space, Renee. I have to give it to him."

"You're both as hard-headed as the other." Renee shook her head and backed away when Brianna tried to return the sandwich. "What else is going on in that stubborn little head of yours, Bri? Tell me."

Brianna gazed out the window to watch a group of kids work in the garden Jackson had tilled for them. Colorful vegetables exploded along the ground and crawled up stakes that were tucked carefully into the soil. Sunflowers soared skyward, heavy with seeds, and already the pumpkins were beginning to turn from deep-green to light orange. A few of the girls had fashioned a scarecrow out of an old flannel shirt and patched blue jeans, complete with a baseball cap and tennis shoes stuffed with straw, and he stood sentinel over the wild array of colors. Brianna remembered the bareness of the ground before Jackson came to till it, and she worried if Thursday's Child was forced to close the garden might meet the same depressing fate as that of her family's following her mom's death.

The thought saddened her to the core.

"Bri?" Renee nudged her shoulder gently. "Are you in there?"

"Yeah. Sorry." She shook her head to clear the memory and focused on the sandwich that was dripping tomato juice onto files strewn across her desk. "Maybe I should have just a bite."

"Yes, you should. And while you're chewing, tell me what's got you so distracted lately."

She nibbled a bit, chewed, and drew a cool sip of bottled water to wash it all down. "It's not just Jackson, or the worry over losing Thursday's Child." She hesitated. Saying the words would make the problem reality. And she didn't know if she had the patience—or the fortitude—to deal with one more problem. She sighed. "It's...Terri, too. She called last night. Things didn't work out as she planned in New York—"

"No surprise there."

"I know. Anyway, she's coming home...soon."

"How soon?"

"She didn't say. It could be today—or next week."

"Have you told Andy?"

"Not yet. I want to be sure she's really going to come. Sometimes she says things and doesn't follow through. And he's going to be..."

"I know. If she *does* get here, it's going to rock his world, good or bad—and from past experience, it'll most likely be bad."

"I hope not. She sounded..."

"How?"

"I don't know. Just...different, calmer." Brianna took another bite of the sandwich, had trouble chewing through the dryness that had taken hold of her mouth. "Do you think she might finally have her head on straight? Do you think...?"

"Anything's possible, Bri. You know that as well as I do." Renee's gaze met hers, held. In the clear green eyes she found the concern of a true friend. "But don't get your hopes up. I don't want to see you hurt again."

"I have to tell Andy...soon."

"Yes, you do...before he finds out from someone else."

****

Jackson wiped beads of sweat from his forehead with the hem of his T-shirt. Two hours until the press conference he'd asked Stan to schedule with ESPN—plenty of time to finish this workout and change into something camera-worthy.

He had things to take care of—unfinished business.

He pedaled harder on the recumbent bike. Pain still laced his knee, but it nibbled instead of gnawing...whispered instead of shouting. He'd heal to play another day—if he wanted.

Stan had bought him an extra week to make his decision. Sure, the wolves in Washington were pacing at the door, but he kept them at bay—for now.

He'd seen another segment for Thursday's Child on the evening edition of Knoxville's Channel Ten News last night. The building's lease was nearly up, and a plea went out for funds to keep the doors open—at least for a while longer. The sight of Brianna—her chocolate kiss eyes bruised with shadows from lack of sleep—made his gut clamp with remorse. There was nothing he could do. He had to be careful to make the right decision.

No way will I hurt her again—ever. I have to take care of things here before I'll be any good to anyone.

The timer beeped, and he slowed the pedals of the bike. His heart raced, but the sweat that pooled along his spine made him feel invigorated and renewed. He slipped off the bike and took his cell phone from his pocket to punch the speed dial.

"Are they set up yet?" he asked Stan.

"The reporters are waiting, just like you asked. They're pacing like caged animals." His voice lowered. "Care to share what you plan to say?"

"You'll hear it when the rest do. Just make sure everything's ready when I get there. I don't want this to take all day."

"I've got it taken care of, Jackson. Now, about signing the contract—"

"Not now, Stan. Let's get the press conference out of the way first."

****

"I won't go with her!" Andy's cry reverberated off the kitchen walls. "You can't make me."

"Nobody's making you go anywhere." Brianna reached for him, but he backed away like a frightened animal. "She's just coming for a visit, that's all."

"That's never all." His voice cracked with the first hints of manhood, and Brianna saw the tears that filled his eyes, heard the pain in his voice, and it tore her to pieces inside. "She'll find a way to mess things up. She always does."

"That's not—" Her voice caught. *That's not true*, she'd begun. But it *was* true. Terri *did* always seem to find a way to throw a wrench into the mix. She tried another tack. "Just give her a chance, will you? She misses you, Andy. She just wants to see you."

"If she really misses me she'd call once in a blue moon."

Brianna cringed. *How can I argue with that?*

"I wish Jackson was here." Andy paced the floor, slapping a hand against his thigh with each step. "He'd know what to do."

She wished it, too. Jackson always did seem to have a way with her sister, even though he was five years younger. He could make Terri laugh when no one else could, and more often than not he'd draw her out of the deep funk she sometimes slipped into without warning in the years following their mom's death.

But he wasn't here, so she'd have to find a way to wade through this mess on her own. Andy was counting on her, and she wouldn't let him down.

"I'm sorry." Brianna drew a sip of lukewarm hazelnut coffee. The brew had cooled while she tried to reason with Andy, and now the once-smooth flavor turned bitter as it raced down her throat. "I should have told you sooner. I just..."

"How long have you known?" His gaze met hers, held, and in his wounded charcoal eyes she found all of her insecurities reflected back.

"A couple of days. But—"

Tears spilled over to slide down flushed cheeks. “You don’t want me here, do you? That’s why you didn’t say anything until now.”

Her heart caught, tore just a bit. “Yes. Oh, Andy, yes, I want you here.” And she realized just how much she’d grown to love him. “Don’t ever think anything different.”

The sound of a car coming up the drive silenced them both. Andy froze still as a block of carved ice.

A car door slammed and Terri’s voice rang out. “Brianna! Andy! Hey, I’m here! Anybody home? Put on a pot of coffee.”

Andy made a sound that was a cross between a whimper and a growl. His eyes grew wide and wild, and he spun on his heel. He flew through the kitchen, past the living room, and the slam of his bedroom door shook the house.

Brianna trembled.

“Hey, sis.” Terri strode through the kitchen doorway. “What’s going on with the kid? Why the fireworks?”

“Hello, Terri.” She crossed her arms and plastered on a lopsided grin. “I thought you were coming tomorrow.”

She shrugged. “What’s a day here or there?” She sniffed the air and settled into a chair at the table. “Is that hazelnut I smell? Pour me a cup, will you?

The interstate is more harrowing than a racetrack. I need to take a load off."

****

Jackson never got used to the glare of the spotlights and the crowd of reporters that seemed bent on shoving microphones into his face as they battled to edge in a question. Most of the questions were sports-related, but a good chunk were personal...and none of their business.

"What's the bottom line, Jackson?" One shouted over the rumbling of the crowd.

"The bottom line is...I'm retiring." A flurry of activity ensued. Questions came like machine gun rapid-fire.

"Is it the knee?"

"Is it because you were traded?"

"What—you don't like Seattle?"

"Is it your father? It's no secret he's been plagued by health problems."

"Is it a woman?"

"Hold up." Jackson raised a hand to silence the crowd. "Give me a minute."

The reporters shifted feet and turned from side to side to gawk at each other. Papers rustled in the breeze coming off the river, and a flurry of nervous coughs pockmarked the air.

"My knee is pretty much healed," Jackson continued when he'd gathered his thoughts. "And I like Seattle well enough...but my heart will always be in Jacksonville. That's where I started my NFL career, and that's where I'd like to end it. As for my dad, he's doing great. I appreciate your concern."

"And the woman?" A reporter jockeyed for position from the rear of the crowd.

"No comment." He plastered on a grin for the flurry of cameras that clicked and whirred. "I'd like to thank all the fans who've supported me so faithfully over the years. It's been an amazing ride. I've been blessed to be a part of this team—this community—for so many years."

"Wait!" The short, stout guy who reported for the Jacksonville Sun nearly skewered him with a microphone. "Is this about the woman you helped with that camp—Thursday's Child, wasn't it?"

Jackson donned his best poker face and cleared his throat. "I have to go now. Thank you all for coming out today."

"Where are you headed, Jackson?"

The question gave him pause. Where would he go next?

He grinned mysteriously at the sea of reporters and kept walking.

I'm not sure where I'll end up, but I know it's not here.

His cell phone vibrated in the pocket of his khakis. He pulled it out to check the caller ID.

Andy.

He pressed the message retrieval and listened to Andy's grief-stricken voice. His heart tumbled, and it became suddenly clear.

Home...to Knoxville. That's where I'm going.

15

HE CAME WHEN I NEEDED him most.

After a week without so much as a word, Jackson had turned the Mustang into Brianna's driveway and rushed up the walk to rap on her front door.

And without waiting for her to open it, he'd bounded right inside.

Brianna had been in the kitchen, scrolling through the contacts stored in Andy's phone. When she glanced up at the sound of his feet pounding he floor, the worried look in his eyes turned her cold inside.

"Is Andy okay?" The question brought everything home. The room swam and Brianna stumbled under the weight of his gaze. She felt him catch her and ease her into a chair.

"Whoa, there." His hands were warm and gentle, his tone coaxing as he brushed tangled hair from her clammy forehead. "Breathe, Brianna."

She couldn't. She began to choke. He splayed a hand between her shoulder blades and patted until the coughing subsided. The scent of him—cherries mixed with a familiar outdoor, woodsy smell—filled her.

"Better?" His gaze found hers when she lifted her head.

"Yes, a little." She drew a deep breath, fought the tickle that rose in her throat once more. The room came back into focus and the clamminess turned to heat. "Jackson, what are you doing here?"

"Andy called me."

"What?" She leapt to her feet. "When?"

"Just before two. He left a message, sounded pretty upset. I'm pretty sure he was crying."

"He's gone." The words came on a sob. "I-I think he ran away."

"You *think*?"

"No. I *know* he ran away."

"Why would he do that?"

Just then, Terri strode in carrying a battered paisley suitcase she'd hauled from the car. "Well, if it isn't Jackson Reed, in the flesh." Her voice rang sickly-sweet. "I heard your interview on the radio. Going to Seattle, huh?"

"What?" He blanched. "No."

"That's not what the local radio station reported."

Brianna's belly felt like a rock had just been dropped into it.

Seattle…as in Washington? That's clear across the country.

"We'll discuss that later." Jackson dismissed the comment as he took the suitcase from her and set it on the floor. "Have you heard from Andy?"

"Not tonight." She shrugged and gave the suitcase a nudge with the toe of a battered stiletto pump. "Where should I put this, Bri?"

"Leave it right there for now." Exasperation rocked her. "Terri, aren't you at all worried about Andy…your *son*?"

"Uh-uh." She gazed at her reflection in the glass of the microwave door and dabbed at the ripe strawberry-colored lipstick she'd just re-applied. "He'll come back. He just does this for attention."

Brianna fought the urge to shake some sense into her sister. "I don't think so."

"You go look for him if you want, but I'm staying here." She leaned against the countertop and smoothed her hair with one hand. "Storm's brewing. It's nasty out there."

"How long has he been missing?" Jackson asked.

Brianna felt wrung out. An onslaught of tears dampened her cheeks. She longed to have him draw her close and soothe away the worry.

"I don't know, exactly." Her voice was thick with grief. "I called him for dinner an hour ago, and when he didn't answer I went in to check on him.

That's when I found his window propped open and he was gone. But he'd been in his room for a while, Jackson. He got upset when..."

"It's my fault," Terri tossed in. "I shouldn't have come back here. This town...I can't stand it."

"There's no point in placing blame." Frustration clouded Jackson's gaze as he glanced at her. The room was filled with the faint odor of stale tobacco that clung to Terri's low-cut rayon blouse and distressed, faded blue jeans. Years of hard drinking and late-night parties had not been kind to her. Streaks of gray-salted hair framed puffy eyes and a mottled complexion. "It's no one's fault."

"Even so..." She picked at her nails, and flakes of blood-red polish fluttered to the floor to sprinkle the tile like confetti.

"It's getting late, and you're right, Terri—a storm's brewing." Jackson eyed the digital clock on the microwave above the stove. The darkness of night pounced in with a vengeance. "We need to find Andy—quick. I've dialed his cell phone a dozen times since he left the message. He won't pick up. All I get is voicemail."

"That's because I found his phone in the flowerbed beneath his bedroom window. It must have tumbled from his pocket when he climbed out and got lodged in the azalea bush."

Jackson brushed a hand across the rough stubble of beard that covered his chin. "Where would he go, Brianna?"

"I-I don't know. I called Brody, and he hasn't heard from Andy since this morning. So I went through the contact list on his phone and dialed each number. No one's heard from him. A bunch of the kids were supposed to play football at the park this afternoon. Andy didn't show up."

"He's done this before." Terri poured a fresh cup of coffee and settled into a chair at the kitchen table. She kicked off her shoes, propped her feet in the chair across from her and sighed. "I wouldn't get so worked up. He'll come back. He always does."

"Aren't you worried?" Brianna's nerves hummed with a mixture of shock and regret. "He's out there somewhere, maybe hurt...at the very least upset and frightened."

Terri took a gulp of coffee and reached for the loaf of wheat bread Brianna kept on the counter. "You have any ham and cheese to go with this bread? I'm famished. I haven't eaten since this morning, and that was just a cold, sorry excuse for a hotdog from the truck stop when I stopped for gas."

"Terri, please."

"A little mayo would finish things off just fine."

Brianna stifled her spiteful reply by pressing a fist to her mouth and turning away. But not before

Jackson saw the tears that blurred her vision, magnifying the worry. He followed her from the room.

"Brianna, wait."

She kept walking, through the doorway and onto the front porch. The air was cool with the impending storm and wind chimes that hung from a shepherd's crook in the flowerbed beside the stairs danced and jangled a cacophonous tune. The scent of lilac mingled with rain, and on the horizon she saw a curtain of the downpour rolling toward them like a dark wave in the sky. Angry clouds tossed and turned like restless giants and wind hissed like a snake wrapping itself around them.

"This is awful, Jackson. I have to find him." Brianna's eyes scanned the storm-veiled Smoky Mountains beyond. "It's been hours. Do you think he's gone very far?"

"No...I don't know. Did he take his bike?"

"I don't—I didn't—" She sprinted to the garage, threw open the door. "No. It's still here. Thank God."

"That's good." Jackson paced the length of the porch. "Would he get into a car with a stranger?"

"I-I don't think so." Her belly roiled as the tears flowed. "Oh, Jackson, I don't know."

"Did he have any money?"

"No. He left his wallet. I found it on his dresser." She sobbed as rain began to splatter the roof, echoing through the garage. “He was wearing shorts and a T-shirt. He doesn’t even have a jacket.”

The wind picked up, ripping through her light cotton T-shirt. Brianna hugged her arms tight to herself, her teeth chattering as a gust of wind forced the first bullets of rain through the open door to bite them.

“Jackson!” Her voice was pleading.

He took her hand and led her toward the driveway. “Let’s get in my car, drive around and see...”

“Okay.” Lightening electrified the evening sky, and Jackson sheltered Brianna beneath his shoulder as he unlocked the Mustang’s door and helped her in. Thunder crashed while he slipped into the driver’s side and cranked the engine. The car rocked as the earth shook around them, and Brianna cried out.

“It’s going to be okay, sweetheart.” He backed down the drive beneath a waterfall of rain. The car’s headlights barely put a dent in the growing blackness and his eyes strained to see through the dark, soupy mess. “Sit back, put your seatbelt on.”

“Be careful, Jackson.” Droplets of water dripped from Brianna’s hair. She shivered under the blast of the defroster that fought to keep the windshield clear. “I’m scared.”

This isn’t happening.

Brianna gazed out the window through a curtain of rain that sluiced down the glass, turning everything to a distorted illusion.

"I don't think he'd come this far," she murmured as Jackson sped over the Henley Street Bridge. "At least, I hope not."

"You're right." He merged over a lane and turned into a nearly-deserted parking lot along Broadway. Traffic had eased, and the lights in the buildings along the road were mere pockmarks—an inhabited office here and there...someone working overtime. Jackson shifted into reverse, turned the Mustang around.

Brianna stole a look at him. Waves of dark, damp hair curled over the nape of his neck and his biceps were taut as his hands clenched the wheel—white-knuckled. Beneath the glow of a streetlight she saw that his jaw was set in a tight line and his gaze seemed to pierce the darkness as he struggled to see down a storm-swept road through the black. The Mustang bounced through a pothole.

"Think, Bri," Jackson gripped the steering wheel. "There must be somewhere he'd go...somewhere he'd feel safe until the anger, the hurt wears off."

"Wait!" She sat up and splayed one hand on the dash in front of her. "Turn here, Jackson. Quick!"

There was one place Andy would go when he felt he had nowhere else to turn—one place he knew he'd be safe.

Thursday's Child.

They turned a corner, and the glare of lights through the expanse of gymnasium windows told her all she needed to know.

"Look, Jackson. He's here. Thank God."

The Mustang skidded in front of the building and they both raced toward the double front doors. Somewhere, in the back of her mind, Brianna realized Jackson had lost his limp. His long, powerful strides overtook hers as they jockeyed down the hall.

The sound of a bouncing basketball reverberated off the walls.

"Andy!"

He looked up at the sound of Brianna's voice and the ball slipped from his hands. For a moment, all three stood stone-still while the ball bounced into a corner, echoing like cannon shot through the nearly-deserted building.

"You came." Andy's gaze slipped from Brianna to Jackson. "You really came."

"Of course I came. You called me, didn't you?" Jackson's voice was filled with the strain of worry coupled with exhaustion. You gave us an awful scare, sport."

"I-I'm sorry." His eyes filled with tears as he dropped his gaze. "I'll bet I'm really in hot water now."

Brianna's heart filled and she felt his hurt as if it was her own. She went to him, drew him in and wrapped her arms around him as sobs wracked his trembling body.

"It's going to be okay, Andy," she soothed. "Whatever happens, we'll make it through."

"Promise?" He wiggled in closer and clung to her as if he'd never let go.

"Yes, I promise."

"I don't want to go to New York, or anywhere else. I like it here."

"No one said you have to leave."

"Not yet, but she will. Mom will."

"Let's just take things one step at a time. Trust me, okay?"

"O-Okay."

Jackson sauntered over to wrap his arms around both of them. His embrace protected, comforted, and soothed away the hurt. The scent of him was so familiar...so very Jackson, that Brianna nearly broke down.

"I think we should go home and talk this out," he murmured as he brushed her hair with his lips. "We need to talk it out—all of it."

"Yes," Brianna smoothed a hand over Andy's flushed cheek to brush away tears as his trembling subsided. “It’s time to stop running away. Let’s go talk it out.”

“You’re gonna ground me for sure now, aren’t you?” Andy swiped huge, round eyes with his forearm.

“A week, at least.”

He groaned. “Man, I really hate cleaning the bathrooms.”

Brianna laughed and patted his back. “You’ll survive it.”

The three walked to Jackson’s car, hand in hand, while a thought played over and over through Brianna’s mind.

Andy found a safe place to vent...at Thursday’s Child.

****

“Is he sleeping?” Jackson asked.

“Out like a light.” Brianna slipped off her sandals and slid into the wicker chair beside him. The storm had cleared and the sky was alight with stars. He offered her a glass of tea, and she took a long drink to ease the ache in her parched throat. “I’ve never seen him cry like that. It was...frightening.”

“It was a long time coming, Bri. I think he just needed to let loose. You can only hold things inside for so long before you blow. I think we both realize that now.”

"Yes...we do." Her gaze found his, and she saw a glimmer of the boy there, the one she'd fallen in love with so many years ago...

...the one I still love.

"I'm not going to Seattle, sweetheart." His voice was rough with pent-up emotion. "I'm not going anywhere but...here." He gathered a strand of her hair and tucked it behind her ear. The brush of his knuckles across her cheek made her shiver. "I second Andy's sentiments on the point...I like it here, too."

"But, Terri said—"

"I never should have left you in the first place, Bri. I had no right saying the things I said to you that night. It was ugly and wrong—*I* was wrong—and foolish."

"I was wrong, too, Jackson, to keep my true feelings from you. I should have never pushed you away. We should have talked about it—talked things out like we did tonight…like we are now. It's not so hard, is it?"

"I didn't leave much room for talking, the way I went on and on about being drafted."

"You worked hard for it. You had a right to be excited…and a touch proud."

"But I got so caught up…beyond anything reasonable. Can you ever forgive me?"

"Can *you* forgive *me*?"

"I already have." His eyes shone bright with truth. "I love you, sweetheart. I'm staying here—for good. No more football...at least not pro." He grinned. "I may be persuaded to toss the ball around with Andy and the kids at Thursday's Child from time to time, and I heard the coaching position at the high school might come available when Mr. Landers retires at the end of this season, but that's it."

She lowered her gaze. "We may not have a Thursday's Child program much longer. The papers came this week, saying we have to move. The building's going up for sale, Jackson. We're done."

"Maybe not." His car keys jangled in his hands. "Wait here."

"Jackson..." She watched him lope down the driveway to the Mustang that was parked behind Terri's beat-up sedan. "What are you doing?"

He returned with a sheaf of papers, grinning like a Cheshire cat. "I've lived my dream, Bri. Now, it's time for you to live yours. We can't let all the kids down, can we?"

Brianna's heart thudded like a base drum as she scanned the first page. "Oh, Jackson, this is a contract to purchase the Thursday's Child building and grounds. But how? When?"

He shook his head, pressed a single finger to her lips. "You'll have to go by the bank, sign a couple of papers. But the rest is done. The building belongs to Thursday's Child now."

Tears filled her eyes. "Oh, Jack...this is more than amazing. It's..."

"Love." He drew her into his arms. "I love you, Brianna Caufield."

She nestled her cheek to his chest, breathed in the familiar, woodsy smell of him. "And I love you, Jackson Reed."

Epilogue

"RENEE," BRIANNA STRODE INTO THE office. "We're gonna need to hire two more summer counselors to keep up with the flow of kids. It's unreal how they just keep coming through the doors—more every day."

"Hire them." Renee tapped a sequence of keys to close the program on her computer screen. She glanced up and grinned. "We've got the funds for a half-dozen more, if we need that many."

"We just might." The words warmed Brianna. Outside the window, sunlight danced and shimmered off the crystal-blue water of the Olympic-sized pool that had been installed over the winter months. In an hour the Channel Ten News Team would arrive to film a ribbon-cutting ceremony.

She watched Jackson run across an expanse of grass along the pool fence, a football cradled in his arms like a baby. Andy chased at his heels while the spunky dark-haired girl named Katie cheered him on. The two had become fast friends since she'd helped him with his bathroom duties the week he was grounded, after running away that long-ago stormy night. Andy came to Jackson's shoulder now, and it wouldn't be long before he rivaled Jackson in height and weight.

It's amazing the difference a year makes.

After a short stint in Knoxville, Terri returned to New York. She thought she might write the great American novel, but quickly found the solitude monotonous and boring and decided to perform in a nightclub instead. Maybe an agent would see her show, and decide to take her along on a ride to the big time. It didn't take much convincing from Jackson to persuade her to leave Andy behind to finish school, which was just fine with Brianna. She'd grown to love Andy as if he were her own...Jackson had, too.

And Jackson, well, he'd found his niche running camps for the kids at Thursday's Child and coaching the high school football team where Andy planned to play next fall. With Jackson's help, he showed a lot of promise. There'd already been talk among the scouts who stopped by for a visit from time to time.

Laughter drifted through the office window on a breeze that held the first hint of summer. The sound filled Brianna's heart and made her smile. She loved Jackson...had loved him from the first time she met him in the school cafeteria when they swapped lunches in sixth grade.

She fingered the diamond on her finger and thought of the wedding bands she and Jackson chose to pair with it when they married next month. The rings were beautiful, solid...a symbol of the promise of their future together.

Dear Reader,

I hope you enjoyed ***Promises Renewed***, and that it encouraged you in your own personal walk with the Lord. You'll find further inspiration and encouragement on The Potter's House Books Website, and by reading the other books in the series. Read them all and be fortified and uplifted!

Find all the books on Amazon and on The Potter's House website.

Book 1: The Homecoming, by Juliette Duncan

Book 2: When it Rains, by T.K. Chapin

Book 3: Heart Unbroken, by Alexa Verde

Book 4: Long Way Home, by Brenda S Anderson

Book 5: Promises Renewed, By Mary Manners

Book 6: A Vow Redeemed, by Kristen M. Fraser

Book 7: Restoring Faith, by Marion Ueckermann

Books 8 – 21 coming throughout 2019

I hope you've enjoyed ***Promises Renewed***. Look for all of the books in the Potter's House collection, including my next, ***Tragedy and Trust***, coming in October. In the meantime, I'd like whisk you away to my cozy small-town series filled with friends, family, faith…and a hint of mystery: ***Diamond Knot Dreams***.

A Tender Season ~

Love blooms in the most unlikely places…

Hattie Cutler and Anthony Moretto have both survived the death of their spouses. With children grown and the Cutler Nursery business flourishing, Hattie decides it's time to turn her attention to other endeavors. A community garden on the church grounds is just the place to start, so she spearheads the project. When Anthony steps in to offer assistance, more than gardening is on the agenda. Can the pair learn to sow beyond than vegetables and, in turn, reap a beautiful future together?

Veiled Gems ~

Lila Brooks believes in fairytale endings for everyone but herself. She coaxes her dream of opening a wedding shop into reality when she commissions Morgan Holt to transform a run-down Victorian house into an all-inclusive bridal boutique, Diamond Knot Dreams. Clover Cove's residents have whispered that the house is filled with spirits, but superstitions have no place in Lila's life.

Morgan Holt spent the better part of his youth transplanted from one foster home to another. Separated from his older brother, Gunnar, at an early age, they're reunited shortly after Morgan's arrival to Clover Cove. But the last thing Morgan wants is to trust his heart again to a family—or a woman as beautiful as Lila Brooks. He has plans to finish work on the Victorian and then ride off into the sunset, a move he's perfected over the years.

Soon Lila and Morgan have a chance at their own Happily Ever After, but will events from the past destroy their future?

Jeweled Dreams ~

When best friend Lila Brooks sends out an S.O.S. for help at Diamond Knot Dreams, graphic designer Avery Lakin heads to Clover Cove. She's planning to stay only a few weeks, but nature photographer Jason Ingram captures her attention. Soon, she finds herself swept up in the beauty of his work…and in him.

Jason Ingram spent his twenties traveling the four corners of the earth as a nature photographer. But tragedy has called him home to Clover Cove. He's determined to share nature's bounty through his photography studio while he focuses on raising his precocious niece, Kenzie. What he doesn't plan on is falling for Avery Lakin.

As strange things begin to happen at Diamond Knot Dreams—rumored to be haunted—Avery and Jason must bond together to get to the heart of the matter.

Precious Fire ~

Claire McLaughlin, weary of running a corporate rat-race, dreams of pursuing her passion to bake sweet confections. So when former college roommate Lila Brooks asks for help with catering services at Diamond Knot Dreams Bridal Boutique, Claire grabs the invitation with both hands.

Ryan Kendrick has returned home to Clover Cove to raise his step-brother following the death of their grandmother. Hired to renovate the Town Square, he rents office space on the second floor of Diamond Knot Dreams and soon succumbs to talented Claire McLaughlin's sweet confections—as well as the blue-eyed beauty herself.

As their romance blooms, so do the shenanigans of Diamond Knot Dreams' meddling spirit, Ellie. Will her antics help to draw Claire and Ryan closer together, or bring the blossoming romance to a grinding halt?

Crystal Wishes ~

As a clothing-buyer-turned-seamstress with an eye for fashion, Skylar Lannigan's hands whisper tender ballads over fabric. She fills a sketchbook with flowing and whimsical designs—including versions of a to-die-for wedding dress for her own wedding day—if she'd only find Mr. Right. She'd once imagined a bright future with Adam Caldwell, until he took off with no explanation.

Adam Caldwell's life has been a series of hairpin curves since the night a tragic accident claimed both his parents and nearly the life of his sister, Faith, as well. When Faith, who's still recovering from her injuries, asks for help selecting a wedding dress, Adam accompanies her to Diamond Knot Dreams. He's soon reunited with beautiful and lively Skylar Lannigan.

Adam would love to rekindle a romance with Skylar, but will events from their past rise up to destroy any hope for a future?

Enjoy this sneak peek at ***A Tender Season***…

A Tender Season
(Diamond Knot Dreams Prequel)

HATTIE CUTLER SIGHED AS SUNLIGHT fingered through wisps of clouds to stroke the grounds of Clover Cove Community Church. She felt at peace in the shadow of a majestic whitewashed steeple that rose to kiss the cerulean blue sky, yet something niggled at her heart—a deep sense of longing she couldn't quite form into words.

There was so much work to be done on the community garden that she, along with the help of a handful of the other parishioners, had broken ground on a few weeks ago. Hattie tugged off her gardening gloves and brushed the palm of one hand along tendrils of hair that tickled her damp forehead. It was easy to forget she was knocking on the door of her mid-fifties…not nearly as young as she used to be. But life had tossed her a generous mix of laughter dappled with love of family that kept her feeling spry as a teenager.

Her children were grown and married…all four of them wed to spouses that would make Rick happy if he were here to see what had become of them. Wyatt and Kami, Reese and Peyton, Maddie and Gunnar, Dillon and Brynn. Two-by-two the branches of the Cutler family tree continued to flourish. Each young couple had begun their own journey into growing a family. Hattie's passel of grandchildren were living, breathing proof of the loving bonds that had been forged by her sons and daughter.

But Rick was no longer at her side to witness the adventure. Had it really been five years since his untimely passing? Hattie could barely believe so many days had come and gone, swept away by the fullness of a busy life. Now, when she thought of Rick she remembered only the happy times they'd shared...not the illness that had cut him to the quick and so ruthlessly claimed him during his prime.

Hattie sat back on her haunches and reached for a bottle of water, pausing as a shadow crossed alongside her.

"Here you go."

Her breath caught in her throat. She'd recognize that voice at any given moment and the rich timbre set her spine to tingling with an odd little dance of anticipation. She turned as the chilled water bottle was placed in her hands and found Anthony Moretto standing at her side. His tall, lean form shielded the sunlight from her eyes while a broad smile warmed her to the very core.

"Hi, Hattie." Callused fingers stroked the length of her forearm before falling away to settle back at his side. He eyed the weeds she'd spent the past hour or so taming, now tangled together in a large plastic bucket at the edge of the plot. "I see you've been quite busy this morning."

"Yes." She twisted the cap from the bottle, drew a generous sip to calm her parched throat, and then swallowed before continuing. "I've been neglectful of the gardening the past few days and had a bit of catching up to do before the weeds take up permanent residence."

"Those weeds can wait their turn." His wink was coupled with a sweet, mischievous grin. "Getting a little sidetracked from the task at hand is more than understandable with a new grandbaby just begging to be cuddled."

"Yes, Wyatt and Kami do make beautiful children together." It warmed Hattie to know she and Anthony shared a trio of grandchildren by way of her son, Wyatt, and Anthony's only daughter, Kami, who'd just celebrated their fourth anniversary. "Little Renee is precious as the day is long."

"She's got her daddy's lungs."

"Amen to that. Kami and Wyatt will surely pay their dues this time around." From the latest report, the newborn had squalled with colic through much of her first week. "Is everything OK, though? What are you doing here?"

"Everything is just fine and I should ask you the same." Anthony took her hand and helped her to her feet. "What are you doing working here all by your lonesome on a beautiful day such as this?"

"I don't mind a little time alone." Hattie brushed grass from her skirt and turned to face him. His dark hair and a smile punctuated by a deep dimple at the center of his chin set her pulse to racing. "Being by my lonesome gives me time to reflect."

Anthony's eyes danced as crinkles deepened at their corners. He skimmed a pair of fingers along her shoulder. "And upon what mysteries of the universe might you be reflecting today, sweet Hattie?"

"Hmmm…" Hattie pressed the tip of one index finger to her chin as she eyed the church steeple that rose into the expanse of early-spring sky like a lighthouse to the lost. She found such comfort at the sight of it…such peace. "Where should I start?"

"At the beginning is always a good place." Anthony draped an arm over her shoulder and she felt a sense of comfort and protection that was found with no one else. The pleasing realization had her heart singing as together, she and Anthony surveyed neat rows of vegetables that had been sown a few weeks ago. Now, the seeds sprouted, their crowns reaching eagerly toward the sun. Winter had been mild and spring yawned along the horizon, waking to warm the earth with its promise of new life. Soon there would come a harvest. Anthony squeezed her shoulder gently. "The grounds are looking spectacular, but I expected no less than that. You are, after all, the master gardener."

"I'm in my element here. Once the vegetables begin to bloom and ripen, the months of harvest that follow will help feed the bulk of Clover Cove's families in need."

"Always thinking of others…that's my Hattie."

My Hattie. The words caused a flutter in the pit of her belly. When had Anthony begun to refer to her as 'My Hattie' and when, exactly, had she begun to both welcome and embrace the tender sentiment?

Hattie shook the dirt from her gloves and dropped them into her gardening carry-all. "I've done all I can here for now, except offer these seedlings a long and generous drink of water."

"I'll take care of that. You've done enough for one day." Anthony took the bucket of weeds and set it beside the carryall. "Leave both of those where they are and I'll load them into your car for you."

"I don't have my car." Hattie frowned as she scanned the quiet, winding boulevard beyond the church grounds. "Gunnar dropped me off a few hours ago on his way to run errands, but he'll head back by as soon as I give him a call."

"There's no need to phone Gunnar." Anthony shook his head slightly. "I'll be your chauffer this lovely afternoon."

"Oh, I don't want to inconvenience you."

"Hattie Cutler, bite your tongue." Anthony waved off the comment with a flick of those broad, callused fingers. “You know better than that. You are never, *ever* an inconvenience to me.”

“But—”

“No need to debate the point. I won’t take no for an answer.” He held a hand, palm up in traffic-cop style, toward her to put a quick end to her protests. “Why don’t you head inside and cool off a bit while I finish things here. Then we’ll talk ice cream.”

“Ice cream?” Hattie smacked her lips as the words registered. She could already taste hot fudge swirled atop a heaping scoop of vanilla bean. “Well, I suppose that’s an offer I can’t refuse.”

“Good. And I’ll add that Fred and Jada have a handle on things over at the pizzeria, so I’m in no hurry to return to work there this afternoon. I thought I might see if I can talk you into having lunch with me *before* we indulge in a sweet treat.”

“Oh, Tony…” Hattie removed the broad-brimmed hat from her head and ran a hand through her windblown hair. “I’m a mess.”

“Nonsense.” He quirked a grin and the dimple along his chin deepened handsomely. “You look just fine from where I’m standing.”

“I don’t know…Maddie might need me at the nursery. This beautiful weather has brought customers out in droves. With Wyatt and Kami tied up with their new little one, things are tight.” Hattie thought of the stock that needed tending, displays waiting to be replenished. “And, as I mentioned,

Gunnar went to check on that Victorian house…the one in town that just sold down the boulevard from his garage. While he was working on her car last week, the new owner mentioned she could use some assistance with the renovations. So Gunnar and Dillon are helping to introduce her to a few people in town who know a thing or two in that arena. They'll familiarize her with the ins and outs of Clover Cove while doing their best to find the help she needs to get the business up and running as quickly as possible."

"No worries about the nursery, Hattie. Maddie is handling things just fine. I stopped by there on my way here, to be sure everything was in order. I knew you'd fret." He grinned, and Hattie delighted in the fact that he knew her so well. She *had* been fretting, yet his words calmed. "Reese is back from deliveries to help Maddie if she gets in a bind and I caught a glimpse of Brynn working on an array of planters, as well. The business ship is sailing along nicely, so to speak. No need to worry over that, Hattie. Things won't fall apart if you take a few hours to relax along the way."

"I suppose…"

"I'll twist your arm if I have to." Anthony winked again, causing the heat along the base of Hattie's spine to spike.

"And I just might let you." Hattie's resolve melted away as Anthony's gaze locked with hers. She pressed a hand to her belly and laughed as it grumbled like a lioness at feeding time. "Yes, the jury has apparently reached a verdict—lunch for both of us, followed by a heaping bowl of ice cream."

****

Anthony watched Hattie retreat through the church doors and into the cheerful respite of the modest, tiled foyer. Her hair bounced in a crown of curls around her shoulders, much like brilliant diamonds dancing beneath the fragrant spring sunshine.

Beautiful…yes, she surely was, both inside and out. He loved the way she called him Tony. No one ever in his life had ventured to use the shortened endearment when referring to him. Anthony…he'd always been Anthony.

Except for when he was with Hattie. She made him feel like a celebrity and the guy next door all rolled into one…special on all counts.

Anthony shook his head as he reached for the garden hose wound around a metal holder at the side of the church's brick out-building. He supposed Hattie Cutler was the only breathing soul in Clover Cove who had not yet clued in to the fact that he'd fallen in love with her. Oh, he continued to drop subtle hints at every bend in the road. Yet, like a fickle salmon, she failed to take the bait.

He'd just have to crank things up a notch or two…try a more direct approach. But that was easier said than done when the last time he'd conjured the nerve to ask a woman on a date was more than thirty-five years ago.

He thought of Lillian and her bright, magnanimous smile. Losing his wife in their twenty-ninth year of marriage had set him reeling, for sure. The days that followed had been tough. He still found it a miracle that he'd returned from the brink of despair fully intact to find glimmers of sunlight filtering through fierce storm clouds. As time passed those clouds had slowly faded, replaced by a ribbon of clear, blue sky.

The ribbon proved to be Hattie. She continued to be a vivacious and lively dynamo that allured him into nothing less than amazement at every turn.

Anthony shook gnarled kinks from the length of hose as he headed back to the garden Hattie had so lovingly helped to sow and immersed herself in tending. Under her tutelage, he had no doubt whatsoever that each plant would flourish. She possessed a green thumb, what many residents of Clover Cove referred to as the magic touch. Cutler Nursery stood as proof of the horticultural gifts God had so graciously bestowed upon Hattie. Couple those endowments with the characteristics of hospitality, service, a deep sense of family, and unending loyalty— Hattie Cutler possessed a presence that bordered on ethereal. Sometimes when he stood at Hattie's side, Anthony felt like the mere flicker of a candle in the presence of a floodlight. What were *his* gifts?

He pondered the thought as he offered seedlings a generous drink. The pizzeria that he'd coaxed to life and nurtured for the past two decades was one consideration. He'd almost lost the business following Lillian's death, but Kami had helped him to revive things and to hang on tight through the storm of depression. Now that the storm had passed, punctuated by the wake-up call of a mild heart attack, he'd taken a step back to reflect on the direction of his life and what God might have in store for him. As the result of much prayer, he'd handed the daily operations to Kami and Wyatt. Together the pair stayed true to the course and the business continued to flourish.

The hard-fought business success afforded Anthony a sense of freedom he hadn't felt in decades. Now, he enjoyed more time to explore other adventures…other interests.

More time for Hattie.

As she crossed the church yard toward him, looking pretty as a summer breeze in her wide-brimmed hat and floral-patterned skirt, Anthony figured there was no better time than the present to fan the flames of romance. Those flames seemed to devour him like a raging inferno whenever Hattie came near.

His gaze slipped to capture Hattie's lithe figure and radiant smile. It was time to reveal to her, once and for all, exactly how he felt about her.

He'd let God take it from there.

****

Hattie nestled alongside Anthony in a wrought-iron bench across from Sweets and Treats Ice Cream Shop. She scooped whipped cream from the top of her hot fudge sundae and spooned it into her mouth, savoring the sugary-rich flavor. It slipped over her tongue and down her throat, forging a delightful trail.

"Delicious." She lifted her gaze to find Anthony staring at her, the wisp of a smile on his full lips. A flashfire of warmth swam over her cheeks as she swallowed hard. "How's yours?"

"Hmm…" Anthony raised his cone of fudge ripple like a torch. "Not as good as yours, judging by those groans of satisfaction."

"Was I…groaning?" Hattie covered her mouth with the palm of her hand and turned her head, hiding the heat of blush that scorched her. "Goodness sakes, if I had a dollar for every time I've made a fool of myself…"

"It's endearing to watch you take such delight in a simple bowl of ice cream." Anthony laughed softly. "You're easy to please, Hattie."

"I'm glad you think so." She ventured another bite of the sundae. "My children would testify to the opposite."

"They're entitled to their opinion, but I beg to differ."

"I'm flattered that you do." A gentle breeze lifted Hattie's hair. Curls tickled the nape of her neck as sunlight dappled the pavement along the sidewalk. The scent of lilacs just coming into bloom mingled with damp earth and sweet grass that shimmered with its first spring cut. "Thank you for lunch and for this delicious ice cream. It's certainly a treat after working away the morning."

"You're welcome. You work too hard, Hattie."

"I could say the same about you. When's the last time you took a vacation?"

"My heart attack?"

"Case in point. You scared the life out of me with that, you know. I thought we'd lost you for good, and I couldn't bear…"

"What couldn't you bear, Hattie?"

"I'd miss you and your linguini with clam sauce."

"Yes, my linguini is soon-to-be world famous." Laughter bubbled up to spill from Anthony's lips. "But I'll share the recipe with you, just in case."

"That's not funny, Tony." Hattie swatted his arm. "You should take a vacation. You *need* and *deserve* a vacation."

"I'll consider it." He squeezed her hand and then lifted his fingers to graze the knuckles along her jawline. "In the meantime, I have something for you."

"More than this?" Hattie gripped the ice cream bowl between her palms. "Isn't lunch and dessert enough?"

"No." He dipped a hand into the front pocket of his jeans and retrieved a small, black velvet box with a silver-toned hinge. "Here you go."

"Oh, Tony…what's this?" Hattie's pulse stammered as he took her hand and turned it palm-up before placing the box there.

"Open it."

Slowly, carefully, she lifted the lid, pulling it back on its hinge. A delicate silver heart caught the sunlight while a light-blue gem at its center winked up at her.

"Is that…?"

"Yes, it's aquamarine, the birthstone for March." He lifted the heart from the box. "It's in honor of Renee's birth on the thirty-first. As you know, she slipped in there right under the wire—two minutes before midnight."

"You shouldn't have." Hattie sat mesmerized by the shimmer of jewelry coupled with Anthony's thoughtfulness. "It's lovely, Tony. Truly it is. I'll treasure it always."

"It matches the others you've collected." Anthony caught the necklace that rested along her collarbone between his fingers. Silver hearts twinkled there, each adorned with a gemstone corresponding to the birth months of her grandchildren. "You have every month's stone with the exception of a diamond."

"Oh, well…" Hattie's fingers brushed his as she touched the small colony of hearts. "No April babies."

"And no worries in that department." Anthony winked at her. "You'll get your diamond. Maybe we should simply forge another route."

****

Hattie's shimmer of tears at the unexpected gift caused Anthony's heart to belly flop in his chest. "I didn't mean to make you cry."

"You're so thoughtful." Hattie lifted her hair as he unclasped the necklace. "They're happy tears because you make me feel like a queen."

"A queen? Well, that's a relief." The soft skin at the nape of her neck ignited a longing Anthony hadn't felt in years. "Because I'd never hurt you, my Hattie. I'd never do anything to cause you sad tears. Never, *ever*."

"I know that, and I take great comfort in the knowledge." She turned slightly and he caught a whiff of her perfume…a subtle blend of scents reminiscent of sweet berries and rain-washed earth. "You're a good man, Tony Moretto. It's a blessing to share a trio of grandchildren with you."

"And I don't think Kami and Wyatt are finished yet in that department—not if Kami has her way." He caught a lock of Hattie's hair and let the silky texture slip through his fingers. "Did you ever imagine God would place that particular bend in the road—the gift of grandchildren—at our feet?"

"No, but it's a wonderful surprise."

"An *amazing* surprise." Anthony threaded the silver heart onto the delicate chain and it tinkled softly against the others. With the greatest care he draped the necklace in place at Hattie's collar and carefully re-clasped it. "That's perfect."

"Yes, it is." Hattie pressed a palm to the growing cluster of hearts and felt the steady *thump-thump* of her own. "It's more that perfect."

"Is that possible?"

"With you it is."

"Well, then…" Anthony took the empty ice cream bowl from her lap and tossed it into a nearby trash can along with the wrapper from his waffle cone. "Would you like to walk a bit? That lunch…"

"Yes." Hattie pressed a palm to her belly. "A stroll is a fabulous idea. The afternoon is gorgeous."

"Come, then." He took her hand and helped her to her feet. "Let's take a look at that Victorian house you mentioned earlier. What type of business does the new owner plan to launch?"

"I'm not sure. Gunnar didn't mention that."

"Perhaps we'll find a clue." Together, they headed toward the boulevard. "In the meantime, may I ask you a question?"

"Sure." Hattie nodded slightly as she shielded her eyes with one hand and tilted a glance his way. "Ask away."

"If you could travel anywhere, Hattie—anywhere in the world—where would you choose to go?"

"Anywhere?" She caught her lower lip between her teeth as she paused to think. "Hmm…that's an easy one. Most women would choose Paris or Rome, or perhaps even somewhere more exotic, I suppose. But I'm captivated by the open waters of the Pacific Ocean. I've always wanted to go on an Alaskan cruise, with towering fjords and miles of sparkling-blue water as a backdrop. I'd love to whale-watch and glimpse an eagle soaring…the whole nine yards."

"Alaska, huh?" Anthony's fingers twined with hers as they crossed the street, nearing the Victorian house. "My Hattie, but you truly *are* easy to please. Are you sure it's not those endless cruise-ship buffets that entice you to head aboard?"

"Well, there's *that*. Though endless lunch and dinner buffets don't top *my* list as I imagine they might yours." She jabbed him playfully in the ribs. "Where would you choose to go, Tony?"

"I'd love to go anywhere you are, even if it's merely the porch swing overlooking your backyard."

"That's beyond sweet."

"And wholly sincere." He lifted her hand and planted a gentle kiss on the tip of each finger. "By the way, have you heard about the Spring Fling the rotary's hosting to raise money for their foreign exchange student program?"

"Yes, I read about it in the Clover Cove Times. A four-course dinner followed by ballroom dancing next Saturday at the civic center."

"Let's get a head start on that dancing." Anthony swung her into a little two-step right there on the sidewalk.

"Oh, Tony!" She pressed one hand to his shoulder while the other wrapped around to his back. "What will the neighbors think?"

"Let's make them jealous." He capped off the move with a twirl and a graceful dip that had Hattie gazing into his eyes as she giggled like a school girl.

"I had heard through the grapevine that you cut a pretty mean rug." He bowed regally. "And from what I can tell it's true."

"The grapevine? Oh, you must mean Kami. We were talking a few weeks ago when I mentioned I like to dance." She waved off the thought as she caught her breath. "But that was a long time ago. I haven't danced in years, Tony—at least not until just now, today."

"You should dance more often, Hattie. With me." He spun her once more, eliciting the light tinkle of laughter. "What better time to start than now? It's true that we're not getting any younger, but I'm not ready to be put out to pasture yet."

"Nor am I." Hattie smoothed a hand through her windblown hair. "But I'm giving you fair warning—dancing with me might prove dangerous. There's a good chance I'll trample your feet."

Anthony couldn't agree more. Dancing with Hattie might prove dangerous, all right, but not for the reasons she'd highlighted.

"I'll wear my steel-toe boots." He laughed and then sobered quickly as he considered his next words. "As for the Spring Fling…I was wondering if you might allow me to escort you, sweet Hattie."

"Escort me…to the dance?" Hattie's chocolate eyes skimmed the length of him as she dipped her chin. "Tony Moretto, are you asking me on a date?"

"I believe I am." He brushed a strand of hair from her cheek and allowed his knuckles to linger along the smooth, warm skin at her jawline. "And I'd also add it's about time, wouldn't you?"

"Yes." Her voice was barely a murmur as she leaned into his touch.

"Do you mean, yes, it's about time?" Anthony cupped her chin and captured her gaze. "Or yes, you'll allow me to escort you?"

"Yes." Hattie squeezed his hand as her plump, glossed lips curved into an impish smile. "And yes."

Anthony longed to claim those lips but patience outweighed impulse. The time would come for kissing…soon.

"Look, there's a business sign." He pointed toward the Victorian where paint peeled from one whitewashed spire and shutters hung like blackened eyes. The place sure could use a facelift, and by all accounts it was about to get its makeover. A placard had been staked in the lawn beside the front stairs. Anthony read its message aloud. "Coming Soon: Diamond Knot Dreams: Your One-stop Wedding Shop."

"Sounds intriguing," Hattie's gaze drifted to the spire. "Like an adventure in the making. Rumor has it that the house took so long to sell because something ethereal lingers there, something not of this world. But now that the property *has* finally transferred to a new owner, I wonder how long it will be before they're up and running."

Anthony planned to find out…and to ask the new owner for a little help with a thing or two in the process.

****

"You're going dancing, Mom?" Maddie squealed with delight as she cradled Katy against her chest. The three-month-old sported a full crown of soft auburn curls—a mirror of Maddie's. It was a good thing the child could sleep through a tornado because vivacious Maddie had two speeds—fast and lightning-quick, coupled with two volumes—loud and LOUD. "Really…you and Mr. Moretto?"

"Tony…yes. I'm certainly not going to dance with myself at this soiree." Hattie pushed through the shop door to step into a We've Got You Covered Boutique. An over-the-door bell chimed merrily as the scent of rose petals welcomed. "Why are you so shocked? You don't think older people like to dance?"

"You're not old, Mom." Maddie followed her into the shop, careful not to let the door swing back on the sleeping baby. "You're just a little…rusty."

"Well, that's about as flattering as stating that I'm ancient." Hattie waggled her fingers in response to the comment. "Thanks for the vote of confidence, honey."

"I didn't mean it that way. Mr. Moretto—Anthony— is really nice, and you two have a lot in common. It could work." Maddie nodded emphatically. "Yes, I definitely sense some light at the end of the proverbial tunnel here."

"We're going dancing." Hattie headed toward a clothing rack along the far wall, where a shimmer of navy stood out among the bright rainbow of fabric. "Not to the altar."

"Speaking of altars, what do you think of that wedding shop going in across the street…Diamond Knot Dreams?"

"I think it will be a boon to our economy. Kami mentioned she plans to head that way soon to speak to the new owner about the possibility of offering some catering through the pizzeria. And I can see Peyton crafting floral arrangements—with Cutler Nursery as the supplier, of course. Gunnar might have a few connections concerning wedding and reception music. He certainly has the proper background with all of his singing and guitar playing at church."

"Yes, he chatted that up a bit last week when he had the chance. There are endless possibilities."

"Speaking of Gunnar, has he had any luck with the private investigator?"

"Not yet. Morgan is sort of like Bigfoot…there've been several mentions of sightings but no one seems to be able to verify his exact whereabouts."

"Well, I hope Morgan materializes soon. It has to be tough on Gunnar to remain estranged from his brother all these years, and through no fault of his own. The sooner they reconnect, the easier it will be to rebuild those bridges."

"I don't know...some bridges aren't meant to be reconstructed. But the not knowing *has* been hard on Gunnar, and we keep praying..."

"I know you do." Hattie emphasized the point with a stiff nod. "The Good Lord will surely answer those prayers. He always does."

"Speaking of prayers, Mom, you never know where a night of fox trotting with Mr. Moretto might lead. You've both suffered more than your fair share of heartache and recovered like champions. And you've both been alone for too long now." Maddie crossed over to stand at her side. "Besides, just look at Gunnar and me. I took the nursery's truck on a delivery ride and *bam*...literally. A crash course in romance and the rest is history."

"That comes as no surprise to me. You rarely do things the conventional way, my dear." Hattie sliced a glance Maddie's way as she stroked wisps of curls from Katy's damp forehead. "That's one of the reasons I love you."

"And I love you too." Maddie leaned in to kiss her cheek. "So I'll add this to my prayer list and I'll keep praying until..."

"You do that. And, in the meantime, I'll continue my quest for the perfect dress." She turned back toward the wall rack to begin her search anew. "After all, the dance is tomorrow. That's little more than twenty-four hours from now."

“Wow, you really know how to clip things close to the quick. And no…not that one, Mom.” Maddie scrunched her nose as Hattie removed the navy dress from the rack and held it up to the mirror. “It’s too stark and way too dark. You’re going to dinner and dancing. You need something light, cheerful and flattering.”

“OK, maybe I *am* a little rusty at this.” Hattie placed the dress back on the rack and took a moment or two to search listlessly through a handful of others before stepping back. “It’s been a while. You give me a suggestion.”

“Sure I will. Let’s see...” Maddie turned a slow three-sixty sweep of the shop, scanning the offerings. A few degrees into the second turn she paused suddenly, gasped, and jabbed a finger toward the window display. “Over there. Do you see the one on that tallest mannequin at the center of the glass?”

“You mean the calf-length lilac with that flowing, chiffon skirt?”

“Yes, that one.” Maddie started that way. “Isn’t it gorgeous?”

“It’s lovely. But do you really think so?” Hattie pressed a finger to her chin, considering. “It’s not too much?”

“Yes, I really think so and no, it’s not too much. It’s perfect…just perfect.” Maddie headed toward the sales associate, tossing one final comment over her shoulder, “Trust me on this one. You’re gonna be a knockout tomorrow night, Mom. Mr. Moretto won't know what hit him."

You can find both ***A Tender Season (Diamond Knot Dreams Prequel)*** and ***The Diamond Knot Dreams Collection*** on Amazon.

ABOUT MARY MANNERS

Where friendships blossom and love blooms…

Mary Manners is a country girl at heart who has spent a lifetime sharing her joy of writing. She has two sons, a daughter, and three beautiful grandchildren. She lives in the foothills of the Smoky Mountains of East Tennessee with her husband Tim, dog Axel, two rescue cats, Colby and Jax, 13 fish and a dozen chickens.

Mary writes stories full of faith and hope. Her books have earned multiple accolades including two Inspirational Reader's Choice Awards, the Gail

Wilson Award of Excellence, the Aspen Gold, the Heart of Excellence, and the National Excellence in Romance Fiction Award.

Mary loves long sunrise runs, Smoky Mountain sunsets, and flavored coffee. She enjoys connecting with reader friends through her website: MaryMannersRomance.com.

More Titles by Mary Manners

Honeysuckle Cove Series

Sunrise at Honeysuckle Cove (Honeysuckle Cove #1)
Beyond the Storm (Honeysuckle Cove #2)
Honeysuckle Cove Secrets (Honeysuckle Cove #3)
Showered by Love (Honeysuckle Cove #4)
Moonlight Kisses (Honeysuckle Cove #5)
Sweet Tea and Summer Dreams (Honeysuckle Cove #6)
Honeysuckle Cove Collection 1: Books 1-6

Diamond Knot Dreams Series

A Tender Season (Diamond Knot Dreams Prequel)
Veiled Gems (Diamond Knot Dreams #1)
Jeweled Dreams (Diamond Knot Dreams #2)
Precious Fire (Diamond Knot Dreams #3)
Crystal Wishes (Diamond Knot Dreams #4)
Diamond Knot Dreams: The Collection

Cooking Up Kisses Collection

Love on a Dare

Snowflakes and Snuggles Collection

Winter Wishes and Snowflake Kisses

Picnics and Promises Collection

A Pocketful of Wishes

Heart's Haven Collection

Dance with Me
Love Notions
Designed by Love
Babycakes

Christmas Novellas

Angel Song
Christmas Wishes...Special Delivery
A Splash of Christmas
A Boulder Creek Christmas
Sugar Cookie Kisses

Novelettes

Starfire
Wounded Faith

Sweet Treats Bakery Series

Kate's Kisses
Grace's Gold

Tessa's Teacakes
Mattie's Meltaways
Sweet Treats Bakery: 4-in-1 Anthology

Lone Creek Ranch Series

Lost in Lone Creek
Lullaby in Lone Creek
Lesson in Lone Creek
Love in Lone Creek

Miracles at Mills Landing Series

Miracles and Mischief
Stolen Miracles
Miracles and Dreams

Willow Lake Series

Whispers at Willow Lake
Warrior at Willow Lake
Wishes at Willow Lake
Wedding at Willow Lake

Wildflowers and Wished Series

Daffodils and Danger
Freesia and Faith

Lilies and Lies
Evergreens and Angels

Sins and Virtues Series

Disguised Blessings
Heartache and Hope
Secrets Unveiled
Labor of Love
Hearts Renewed
Wants and Wishes
Songs of the Soul

Pure Amore

Blackberry Ridge
Simple Blessings

Stand-alone Titles

Buried Treasures
Wisdom Tree

Thanks for spending a little time with Jackson and Brianna in ***Promises Renewed***. If you enjoyed your time with them, please consider leaving a short review on Amazon. Positive reviews and word-of-mouth recommendations honor an author while also helping fellow readers to find quality fiction to read.

Thank you so much!

If you'd like to receive information on new releases, please follow me on Amazon and at my website: MaryMannersRomance.com.

74483245R00149

Made in the USA
Middletown, DE
27 May 2018